Edmund Goldsmid

A Bibliographical Sketch of the Aldine Press at Venice

Edmund Goldsmid

A Bibliographical Sketch of the Aldine Press at Venice

ISBN/EAN: 9783337097264

Printed in Europe, USA, Canada, Australia, Japan

Cover: Foto ©Raphael Reischuk / pixelio.de

More available books at **www.hansebooks.com**

The Aldine Press.

Bibliotheca Curiosa.

A BIBLIOGRAPHICAL SKETCH

OF

THE ALDINE PRESS

AT VENICE,

FORMING

A CATALOGUE

*Of all Works issued by Aldus and his successors,
from 1494 to 1597; and a list of all known
Forgeries or Imitations,*

TRANSLATED AND ABRIDGED FROM

ANT. AUG. RENOUARD'S

"*Annales de L'Imprimerie des Aldes,*"

AND

REVISED AND CORRECTED

BY

EDMUND GOLDSMID, F.R.H.S., F.S.A.(Scot.)

IN THREE VOLUMES.
VOL. I.
ALDUS MANUTIUS.

PRIVATELY PRINTED, EDINBURGH.

—

1887.

INTRODUCTION.

IN the following pages I claim no greater merit than that of a diligent compiler. With such a work as Renouard's "Annales de l'Imprimerie des Aldes" as a guide, all I have had to do has been to verify his facts, examine such objections as Brunet and other bibliographers have raised against his conclusions, and then state what I myself believe to be the truth, moulding the whole into as readable a form as I could, and endeavouring to make my Catalogue (for it is little more) as little tedious and technical as was con-

sistent with the main object I had in view,
viz.: to produce a handy guide for the use
of the librarian and bibliophile. How far
I have been successful, I leave others to
judge.

The *form* I have given this Catalogue
differs from Renouard's. I have given
a short narrative of the lives of Aldus
Manutius the Elder, Paulus Manutius,
and Aldus Manutius the Younger, in-
serting notices of the works printed by
them in chronological order, while the
Index at the end of Vol. III. will enable
the reader to refer at once to any par-
ticular work he may desire to obtain
information about.

EDMUND GOLDSMID.

EDINBURGH, *January* 1887.

THE ALDINE PRESS.

A LDO MANUZIO, or, in the Latinised
and better-known form, Aldus Manutius, was born in 1447, in the small
town of Bassiano, near Velletri, for he
calls himself *Manutius Bassianas* both in
the *Thesaurus Cornucopiæ* of 1496 and in the
Aristotle of 1495-97, and the word *Bassianas*
is explained by Aldus the Younger, his grandson, in No. 4 of his *Quæsiti per Epistolam*, 1596,
when, writing to Cardinal Niccolò Gaetano,
he informs him that he is led to dedicate his work
to him, because his grandfather's native place
belonged to the family of Gaetano : " Quod autem
majus, quam avum ex eo loco cui familia tua jus
dicit, avitoque imperio præses, originem ducere."
The Cardinal was Prince of Sermonetta, in which
principality Bassiano was situated. Renouard
attributes the fact of Aldus having changed his
designation from *Bassianas* to *Romanus* to the

comparative obscurity of Bassiano, which led him
to adopt the name of the nearest large city, the
greatest of ancient or modern times.

From his own account, it appears that the per-
son to whom his father intrusted his education
was an ignorant pedagogue, who made him learn
off by heart the barbarous verses of the *Doctrinale*
of Alexander de Villa-Dei, supposed to inculcate
the principles of the Latin grammar, though in
reality ridiculous and often unintelligible nonsense.
It was, however, the only elementary book of
instruction in this branch then in use, and bitter
was the lot of the youth of those days who had
not at his elbow an intelligent master to expound
its obscure mysteries! Aldus ever remembered
the tortures his brain had suffered when poring
over Villa-Deis' grammar, and one of his first
works was the composition of a Latin grammar,
first printed by him in 1501, and since often reprinted, which soon drove his old enemy into
well-merited oblivion. It is, of course, wanting
in the precision and analytical method of modern
days, but Aldus, as a grammarian, has the same
merit as is universally conceded to him as a typo-
grapher, of having enabled those who followed
him to do better than himself. A few years later
he went to Rome, where he studied under that
peregregius grammaticus (as he calls him in his
preface to the Hesiod of 1495), Caspar of Verona,

and Domizio Calderino. (See preface to Statius of 1502).

Under these celebrated professors, he made rapid progress in the study of Latin, and was soon named tutor to Alberto Pio, Prince of Carpi, nephew of John Picus of Mirandola. A warm friendship sprang up between master and pupil, which lasted throughout their lives, and amongst various privileges conferred on Aldus, we find the Prince in 1503 authorising him to add to his name the name of Pio. From that time Aldus always calls himself *Aldus Pius Manutius Romanus.* The Prince seems to have resided near Ferrara, where Aldus attended the lectures of Giovanni Guarini, who then filled the chair of Greek in that city. How he profited by his lessons may be gathered from his numerous editions of Greek authors and from his Greek Grammar, which, even now, has a certain value.

In the year 1482 Ferrara was threatened by the Venetian army, and Aldus withdrew to Mirandola, under the protection of his pupil's uncle, "quod et amaret literatos viros, et faveret ingeniis," as he writes to Polizianus in 1485. Picus certainly conferred great favours on Aldus, and, in 1488, advanced him the necessary funds to start a press at Venice, this city appearing to offer the greatest advantages, from its love of Arts and Literature. The date is fixed by Aldus himself, in the preface to the *Aristotelis Organum* of 1495, as he says it is then the seventh year he has been engaged in the difficult and expensive operation of establishing a press. The first work printed by him was

1. -MUSÆI Opusculum de Herone & Landro quod & in latinam linguam ad uerbum tralatum est. *Græce et latine.* 4to.

Collation: For the Greek, 10 leaves (Sigs. A to Aiiiij);—For the Latin, Title-page, and 11 leaves (Sigs. Bij to Bvj). These 22 leaves are generally bound so that the Latin faces the Greek. Some copies have on the second and third Latin leaves the sigs. C and Cij.

This edition of Musæus is not only the first work of Aldus as a printer, which is proved by the preface to the 8vo. edition of 1517, but also the *Editio Princeps* of the poem itself, the Florence edition, 4to, no date, printed by Alopa in capitals, having only appeared after the *Anthologia* of 1496, in the preface to which Lascaris speaks of the use of capitals for the text as an advantageous innovation, whilst it evidently preceded the Greek Grammar of Lascaris, issued by Aldus in 1494. It was printed early in the latter year. It is one of the very rarest of the productions of the Venice press. From a literary point of view, however, the Florence edition is the best. (See Matth. Rover's edition of Musæus, Leyden, 1737).

The Musæus was soon followed (in February 1494-5) * by

2. CONSTANTINI Lascaris Erotemata, cum interpretatione latina, etc. 4to,

This being the first work printed by Aldus with a date, which occurs in the colophon :

Finis Compendii octo orationis partium & aliorum quorundam necessariorum Constantini Lascaris Byzantii uiri doctissimi optimique. Impressum est Venetiis summo studio: literis ac impensis Aldi Manucii · Romani Anno ab in Carnatione Domini nostri IESV Christi. m. cccc. lxxxxiiii Vltimo Februarii. et Deo gratias.

Collation: Title-page, at back of which occurs the preface, which is continued on second leaf. The Text begins on the back of this leaf, and continues to sig. S, on the last page of which is the above colophon. Then comes another series of three signatures, A B and C, containing a preface of Aldus *Ad Studiosos*, an *Alphabetum Græcum, Oratio Dominica, Carmina aurea Pythagoræ*, &c. &c., all of which are mentioned on the title-page, and are therefore part of the work, though the last page of sig. C has

---

* See note on page 16.

VALETE. VENETIIS. M.
CCCC. LXXXXV.
OCTAVO
MARTII.

which proves that the book, though dated in former colophon 1494, really appeared in 1495. This is again followed by two leaves, not included in the register of signatures, containing *errata* and a passage from *Moscopulus*. [*Register:* A—R in fours, S in twos, A—C in fours, 2 leaves *not* included in register.]

Renouard thinks the *Lascaris*, the type of which was extremely rude, and was never again used, except for a few lines in the first volume of the *Aristotle* of 1495, was the first work begun by Aldus, but that the *Musæus* was undertaken, and, being very short, was completed while the *Lascaris* was passing through the press. This view I quite agree with.

Panser (vol. iii., p. 378) mentions a copy of which sig. S must have been reprinted, as the colophon, instead of occupying six lines, as is usual, takes up fourteen lines, and bears the date

Anno ab incarnatione Dni nri IESV xti. m. cccclxxxxv. ultimo Februarii.

The *Lascaris* no doubt proved a profitable undertaking, for it appears from the preface that the first edition of the work (Milan, 1476, folio) had already become scarce. The Aldine edition is now, however, rarer than the *Editio princeps*.

For some years Aldus had been preparing an edition in Greek of the works of Aristotle. It is difficult to picture to one's self the gigantic labour involved in such an undertaking. The mere deciphering of such a mass of ancient manuscripts, many unintelligible or disfigured through the ignorance of the scribes, and no two copies agreeing in their readings, must have presented such difficulties that we can only wonder at and admire the courage of him who first undertook such a task. And when we remember that Aldus did this not only in the case of the five volumes which form his collection of the works of Aristotle, but also in the numerous editions of Greek authors which he afterwards produced, we cannot be astonished that a few errors should have crept in, a few readings should appear doubtful, which later editors, lighted on their way by the lamp he had lit, have been enabled to rectify since his day. The first volume of the collected works appeared with the title:

3. ORGANON Aristotelis (hoc est logici ac dialectici libri.) *Græce.* Folio.

The date appears in the colophon (on last page but one):

Impressum Venetiis dexteritate Aldi Manucii Romani. Calendis Nouembris m. cccc. lxxxxv.

Collation : 234 leaves, without pagination or catch
words, but with signatures.

The four last volumes did not appear till 1497-
98. Aldus was assisted in his work by Alexander
Bondinus (*Agathemerus*), and the volume was
dedicated to his former pupil, Alberto, Prince
of Carpi. To each volume Aldus has prefixed a
preface, and to understand the plan of the work,
these should be read. Indeed, all his prefaces
are worth reading: some on account of the information they give as to the method adopted by
the editor; others for the scraps of valuable
knowledge imparted as to the lives and manners
of the principal literary men of the 15th century.
Complete copies of the Aristotle are scarce. A
fine copy on vellum is in the Bibliothèque Nationale
at Paris.

Two months later, in January 1495-6,* Aldus
produced

4. THEODORI (Gazæ) Introductionæ
gramatices libri quatuor. Eiusdem de
Mensibus opusculum . . . Apollonii
grammatici de constructione libri quatuor.
Herodianus de numeris. *Græce.* Folio.

The colophon reads :

Impressum   Venetiis   in   ædibus   Aldi

---

* See note on page 16.

Romani octavo Calendas Ianuarius. M. cccclxxxxv. Concessum est eidem Aldo ab illustrissimo Senatu Veneto ne cui hunc librum liceat imprimere sub pœna ut in gratia.

Collation: 198 leaves.

This edition is extremely rare, containing, as it does, the *editiones princepes* of all four authors, but at the same time very incomplete, in so far as regards the treatise of Apollonius, *De Construc-tione.* This Apollonius, surnamed ΔΥΣΚΟΛΟΣ (morosus), was the father of Herodianus, whose work follows in the same volume, and taught at Alexandria under Adrian, coming to Rome under Marcus Aurelius. Junta issued an edition of the *De Constructione* in 1515, 8vo, as incomplete as that of Aldus. The first complete edition is that of Frankfort, 1590, 4to.

In February were published

5. THEOCRITI Eclogæ triginta, &c.

Colophon:

Impressum Venetiis characteribus ac studio Aldi Manucii Romani cum gratia, etc. M. cccc. xcv. Mense Februario. Folio.

Collation: 140 leaves without pagination, but with signatures.

The edition is very rare, and is the first of

almost all the works it contains. In Reiske's Theocritus, p. vii., will be found a list of differences noted by Reiske in two copies of this edition. Renouard concludes that signatures Z F and Θ G were reprinted with certain corrections. There are many emendations in the second impression, but it may be at once distinguished by the last page of sig. Θ G having a piece of verse on the death of Adonis, while the original is blank. Of the two impressions the first is the rarest, the second the best.

The year 1495, old style,* closed with the publication of Aldus's first entirely Latin work,

6. PIETRI Bembi de Aetna ad Angelvm Chabrielem liber.

Colophon :

Impressum Venetiis in Ædibus Aldi Romani mense Febrvario Anno. M. VD. 4to.

Collation: 60 pages, with signatures A to D.

This pamphlet is as beautiful as it is rare, Aldus having thrown aside the rude type used in the *Musæus.* as well as the still ruder employed in the *Lascaris.* The text begins on the first page.

---

* It must be remembered that the Old Calendar made the year begin in March and end in February, so that November 1495 was three months *earlier* than February 1495.

Renouard considers that one other work was printed by Aldus in 1495, viz. :—

7. ALEXANDRI Benedicti Pæantii Diaria de Bello Carolino. 4to.

These sheets bear no date, but are printed with the same type used for the *Bembi Aetna* of 1495. It does not seem to me, however, that the type is so new in the *Diaria* as in the *Aetna*, and as the latter is dated at the end of 1495, I would rather attribute the former to the year 1496.

In 1496 Aldus produced, so far as we know, but one book, viz.:—

8. THESAVRVS Cornucopiæ. & Horti Adonidis. *Graece.* Folio.

The colophon reads :—

Venetiis in domo Aldi Romani summa cura: laboreq: præmagno. Mense Augusto. M. IIII. D. Ab Ill. Senatu. V. concessum est nequis &c. ut in cæteris. Vale qui legeris.

Collation : 280 leaves in all.

This is a fine edition, well printed, and extremely rare.

In 1497, the productions of Aldus's press increase considerably in number. We have

9. ΨΑΛΤΗΡΙΟΝ. (Psalterium graecum

B

cura Iustini Decadyi)—*Venetiis*, *Aldus Manutius*. 4to.

Collation : 150 leaves in all.

This rare Psalter is printed in red and black.

10. ARISTOTELIS operum volumen secundum. *Graece*.

Aristotelis uita ex laertio. Eiusdem uita per ioannem philoponum. Theophrasti uita ex laertio. Galeni de philosopho historia. Aristotelis de physico auditu, libri octo. De cœlo, libri quatuor. De generatione & corruptione, duo. Meteorologicorum, quatuor. De mundo ad alexandrum, unus. Philonis iudæi de mundo, liber unus. Theophrasti de igne, liber unus. Eiusdem de Ventis liber unus. De signis aquarum & uentorum, incerti auctoris. Theophrasti de lapidibus, liber unus. *Graece*. — In fine : *Excriptum Venetiis manu stamnea in domo Aldi manutii Romani, et graecorum studiosi. Mense Februario. M. iiid.* Folio.

Collation : xxxii. and 268 leaves.

11. — Volumen tertium. De historia libri novem. De partibus libri quatuor. De incessu liber unus. De motu liber unus. De generatione animalium libri

quinque. De anima libri tres. Parva
naturalia &c.—In fine : *Venetiis in domo
Aldi Mense Ianuario m iiid.* Folio.

Collation : 458 leaves, numbered 1 to 457, with
an added leaf, repeating sig. P P between leaves
400 and 401 ; then 1 blank leaf, followed by
8 unnumbered leaves containing fragments of
Book X de Historia Animalium. These are
often wanting.

12. — Volumen quartum. Theophrasti
de historia plantarum, libri decem. Euisdem de causis plantarum, libri sex. fol.
226. Aristotelis problematum, sectiones
duo de quadraginta. fol. 116. Alexandri
aphrodisiensis problematum, libri duo.
fol. 42. Aristotelis mechanicorum, liber
unus. fol. 12. Eiusdem metaphysicorum,
libri quatuordecim. Theophrasti metaphysicorum, liber unus. fol. 121. *Graece.*
Folio.

The colophon reads :

*Excriptum Venetiis in domo Aldi
Manutii Calendis Iunii M. iii d. Et
in hoc impetratum est &c.*

Each tract is separately paged.

13. INSTITVTIONES graecae Grammatices. (auctore fratre Vrbano Bolzanio
ordinis minorum). — In fine : *Venetiis in*

ædibus Aldi Manutii Romani. M. iiid. mense Ianuario. Impetrauit ab. Ill. S. V. & in hoc qd in cæteris suis. 4to.

Collation: 212 leaves.

These volumes form the second, third, and fourth of Aristotle's works, the first of which appeared in 1495. The fourth volume is very rare. Even in 1499 Erasmus, in one of his letters, says he could not get a copy. Bolzanius or Bolzani was born at Belluno, and assisted Aldus in many of his Greek editions.

14. INDEX corum, quæ hoc in libro habentur.
Iamblichus de mysteriis Aegyptiorum. Chaldæorum, etc. *Latine.* — In fine : *Venetiis mense Septembri. M. iiid. In ædibus Aldi.* Folio.

Collation: 185 leaves ;—1 blank leaf.

Rare.

15. DICTIONARIUM græcum copiosissimum secundum ordinem alphabeti cum interpretatione latina. Cyrilli opusculum de dictionibus, quæ uariato accentu mutant significatum secundum ordinem alphabeti cum interpretatione latina. Ammonius de differentia dictionum per literarum.—In fine : *Venetiis in ædibus*

*Aldi Manutii Romani, Decembri mense. m.
iiid. et in hoc quod in cæteris nostris ab.
Ill. S. V. concessum nobis.* Folio.

Collation : 243 leaves ;—1 blank leaf.

A beautiful book, and exceedingly rare.

16. LAURENTII Majoli liber cui
titulus Epifilides.—In fine: *Impr. Venetiis
in domo Aldi Romani mense Iulio. M.
iiid.* 4to.

A copy of this rare book is in the Sapientia
library at Rome.

17. LIBELLUS de Epidemia, quam
uulgo morbum Gallicum uocant.—In fine :
*Venetiis, In domo Aldi Manutii. Mense
Iunio. M. iii. d.* 4to.

Collation : 29 leaves, the last often wanting.
This is the first book printed relative to this
disease. It was written by Nicolaus Leo-
nicenus. It is very rare.

18. HORAE beatiss. uirginis secundum
consuetudinem romanæ curiæ. Septem
psalmi pœnitentiales cum Letaniis et
orationibus, &c. *Graece.*—* In fine :

* With very few exceptions, the imprint of all
Aldine editions is at the end of the volume, *not* on
the title page. In future, therefore, I shall merely
quote the colophon after the title, omitting the words,
In fine.

Venetiis, Aldus Manutius, 1497, die v. mensis Decembris. 8vo.

Collation: 112 leaves. This book, like all ancient *Horæ*, is extremely rare.

In 1498, only four works seem to have issued from the presses of Aldus, viz.:

19. ARISTOTELIS quintum et ultimum uolumen. *Graece.* Ethicorum ad Nicomachum, libri x. Politicorum, libri viii. Oeconomicorum, libri ii. Magnorum moralium, libri ii. Moralium ad Eudemum, libri viii. — *Venetiis. m.iid. Mense iunio. Apud Aldum. et hoc cum priuilegio.* Folio.

Collation: 317 leaves. This volume completes the *Editio princeps* of Aristotle.

20. ARISTOPHANIS Comoediae Novem. Plutus. Nebulæ Ranæ Equites Acharnes Vespæ Aues Pax Contionantes (*graece cum scholiis graecis, et praefatione graeca Marci Musuri).—Venetiis apud Aldum. m. iid. Idibus Quintilis. In hoc dem quod in aliis nostris impetrauimus.* Folio.

Collation: viii. and 339 leaves;—1 blank leaf. *Editio princeps.* Beautifully printed.

21. OMNIA opera Angeli Politiani, et alia quædam lectu digna.—*Venetiis in*

ædibus Aldi Romani mense Iulio m. iid.
Folio.

Collation: 452 leaves.   The last sig. *K* is blank.
The conspiracy of the Pazzi is omitted, probably because Aldus feared to irritate the
court of Rome by reprinting a history in
which a Pope appeared as an accomplice in a
premeditated murder.

22.   IOANNIS Reuchlin Phorcensis
ad Alexandrum Sextum Pontificem Maxi-
mum pro Philippo Bauariæ Duce Palatino
Rheni, Sacri Romani Imperii Electore
Oratio. VII. Idus sextiles. anno. M. II. D.
Romæ.—*Venetiis Calend. Septemb. m. iid.
in ædibus Aldi Manutii*,   8vo.

Mentioned by Renouard as being extremely
rare.

Besides these works, Aldus issued a catalogue
in 1498, which is extremely curious, as the
prices at which Aldus sold his books are given.
Only *one* copy of this catalogue, as well as of the
catalogues of 1503 and 1513, is known to exist.
It was discovered in a Greek manuscript (No.
3064) in the Bibliothèque Nationale of Paris.   On
the back of the Catalogue of 1513 is written, it is
believed, by Francis d' Asola : "Il primo Indice
de la bona anima di M. Aldo."   These catalogues
are reprinted in full in the appendix to vol iii, of
this work.

In 1499, five works appeared, viz.:

23. EPISTOLARUM græcarum Col-
·lectio. , *Graece.—Venetiis apud Aldum
mense Martio. m. id. cum priuilegio ut in
cæteris.*

2 parts in 1 vol., 4to.

Collation: Part i., 138 leaves.—Part ii., 266
leaves. A rare edition.

24. NICOLAI Perotti Cornucopiæ,
siue linguæ latinæ commentarii, ubi quam
plurima loca, quæ in aliis, ante impressis,
incorrecta leguntur, emendata sunt. etc.
*—Venetiis. In Aedibus Aldi. Mense Iulio.
mid. cum priuilegio.* Folio.

Collation: xxvi. and 642 pages. *Editio princeps.*

Extremely rare.

25. IULII firmici Astronomicorum
libri octo integri, et emendati, ex
Scythicis oris ad nos nuper allati. Marci
Manilii astronomicorum libri quinq;.
Arati Phænomena Germanico Cæsare
interprete cum commentariis et imagini-
bus. Arati eiusdem phænomenon frag-
mentum Marco. T. C. interprete. Arati
eiusdem Phænomena Ruffo Festo Auienio
paraphraste. Arati eiusdem Phænomena
græce Theonis commentaria copiosissima

in Arati Phænomena græce. Procli Diadochi Sphæra græce. Procli eiusdem
sphæra Thoma Linacro britanno interprete.—*Venetiis cura, et diligentia Aldi
Ro. Mense octob. m. id.* 2 parts in 1 vol.
Folio.

Collation : vi. and 370 leaves.

26. PEDACII Dioscoridis Anabarzei
de materia medici libri sex. De Alexiphar-
macis et Theriacis libri tres, septimi,
octavi et noni nominibus insigniti.
Nicandri Colophonii Theriaca et Alexipharmaca, cum scholiis. *Græce—Venetiis
apud Aldum. Mense Iulio. m. id.* Folio.

Collation : vi. and 178 leaves. The title given
above is wholly in Greek.

27. HYPNEROTOMACHIA Poliphili,
ubi hvmana omnia non nisi somnivm esse
docet. atqve obiter plvrima scitv sane
qvam digna commemorat. — *Venetiis
Mense decembri. m. id. in aedibus Aldi
Manutii, accuratissime.* Folio.

Collation : 234 leaves.

An extraordinary book, written in Italian, in-
terspersed with manufactured words from the
Greek, Hebrew, etc. It contains many woodcuts,
attributed to Andrea Mantegna. The author was

Francis Columna, and is revealed in a quaint fashion. By taking the 38 initial letters of the 38 chapters in the work, we find the following sentence :—*Poliam frater Franciscus Columna peramavit.* Columna was a Venetian monk, who died in 1525, aged over 80. The plate of the sacrifice to Priapus, sig. *M.*, being somewhat free, is often wanting. The work is very rare, and fetches a high price.

The year 1500 only produced two books :

28. T. LVCRETII Cari, libri sex nvper emendati. — *Venetiis, accuratiss. Apud Aldum, mense Decem. M. D.* 4to.

Collation : vi and 102 leaves.

Very inferior to the edition of 1515, but scarce.

29. EPISTOLE devotissime de Sancta Catharina da Siena. — *Stampato in la Inclita Cita de Venetia in Casa de Aldo Manutio Romano a di xv Septembrio. M. cccc.* Folio.

Collation : x and 414 pages.

Extremely scarce, especially in good condition, having been much read by the nuns of the day. It is beautifully printed on splendid paper.

With the year 1501, we enter on a new epoch in the annals of the Aldine Press, for it is in this year that the celebrated *italic* first makes its appearance. But before referring to it in detail I must mention :

30. POETAE Christiani veteres, 1501-2. *Venetiis apud Aldum mense Ianuario.* —*M. DI.* 2 vols. 4to.

The first Volume's title page begins :

PRVDENTII POETAE OPERA.

the second

QVAE HOC LIBRO CONTINENTUR.

Sedulii mirabilium diuinorum, &c.

This book is the first in which Aldus used his celebrated mark of the anchor. He had long meditated adopting it, for, at the end of the collection of old astronomers published in 1499, he says, "Sum ipse mihi optimus testis, me semper habere comites, ut oportere aiunt, Delphinum et Anchoram. Nam et dedimus multa cunctando, et damus assidue." And on page *d* 7 of the Polyphilus of the same date, at the foot of one of the quaint wood engravings, will be found this emblem. The first mark adopted is a plain anchor, somewhat square at the bottom, with a dolphin twisted round it, and the name ALDVS printed in two syllables, one on each side. In some of his early books the same mark is surrounded with a border. In 1540 his sons had it re-engraved, the anchor being more rounded at the bottom, and the dolphin not clinging so closely to it. In 1546, it became far more elaborate, an ornament of flowers, cupids, &c., surrounding it, and the words being changed to Aldi Filii. In 1555, Paulus Manutius having become sole master of the establishment, returned to mark No. 2, sometimes surrounded with an oval border. The Emperor Maximilian having granted to Paulus Manutius certain arms in which the anchor and dolphin appeared, Aldus the younger adopted them as his typographical mark, which he used till 1581. After that date we find none but the old No. 2 used.

After this extremely rare collection of Christian poets, Aldus published :

31. PHILOSTRATI de uita Apollonii Tyanei libri octo. Iidem libri latini interprete Alemano Rinuccino florentino. Eusebius contra Hieroclem quem Tyaneum Christo conferre conatus fuerit. Idem latinus interprete Zenobio Acciolo florentino ordinis prædicatorum. *Venetiis in ædibus Aldi mense februario. M. D II.* Folio.

Collation : 143 leaves.

Three dates appear on this volume, 1501, 1502, and 1503. It was probably issued in parts in these years. Some large paper copies are known.

32. VERGILIVS.—*Venetiis ex aedibvs Aldi Romani mense aprili.* M. DI.   8vo.

Collation: 228 leaves.

This is the first work printed by Aldus with his celebrated italic type. It is said that Petrarch's writing first suggested this form, and that the designer and engraver was Francis of Bologna, who had designed and engraved all his previous founts. However this may be, and the verses at beginning of the virgil of 1501, " In Grammato-glyptæ laudem" seem to me to prove the fact beyond all question, this little italic caused a revolution in printing, for, notwithstanding special privileges granted to Aldus by Pope Alexander VI, by the senate of Venice, and other sovereigns and republics, imitations sprang up at Fano, in the duchy of Urbino ; at Florence, where the Giunti, however religious they might be, cared little for ecclesiastical thunders in purely commercial matters ; at Lyons, Basle and other places.

This book is extremely rare.—Three copies on vellum are known : one in the British Museum, one belonging to Lord Spencer, and one that belonged to Mr. Woodhull. Though precious on account of its rarity, it is far surpassed, as a literary work, by the edition of 1514. Seven other works appeared in the same year.*

---

* See also under *Doubtful Editions,* in Vol. iii.

33. NONNI Panopolitæ Paraphrasis Evangelii secundum Ioannem. *Graece.* 4to.

Collation : 51 leaves, without title page.

That this book was published in 1501 is proved by a statement of Aldus himself on the last page of his *Greg. Naz. Carmina* of 1504. Very rare.

34. HORATIVS. — *Venetiis apvd Aldvm Romanvm mense Maio.* M. DI. 8vo.

Collation : 143 leaves ;—1 blank leaf.

As rare as the Virgil of the same date. Copies on vellum are in the British Museum and Spencer libraries.

35. LE COSE volgari di Messer Francesco Petrarcha. — *Impresso in Vinegia nelle case d' Aldo Romano, nel anno.* M DI. *del mese di Luglio.* 8vo.

Collation: 189 leaves.

The four last leaves, containing a long epistle of Aldus, with an errata, were published after the volume had been issued, and are therefore often wanting. It is the first Italian book printed by Aldus. Very rare.

36. JVVENALIS.   PERSIVS. — *Venetiis in ædibus Aldi. Mense Augusto.* M. DI.

Collation: 76 leaves.

There are two editions bearing the same date. One, without the anchor; the other with. This last is evidently the second, as the imprint reads:

Venetiis in aedibus Aldi, et Andreæ Soceri. Mense Avgvsto M. D. I.   8vo.

And Andrea d'Asola only became partner with Aldus in 1508, as we shall see later.

37. MARTIALIS.—*Venetiis in aedibvs Aldi, mense Decembri.* M. DI.   8vo.

Collation: 192 leaves.

Several copies on vellum are known.

38. GEORGII Vallae Placentini Viri Clariss.   De expetendis, et fvgiendis rebvs opvs, in qvo haec continentvr, etc.—*Venetiis in aedibvs Aldi Romani, impensa, ac stvdio Ioannis Petri Vallae filii pientiss. mense Decembri.* M. D. I.   2 vols.   Folio.

Two splendid volumes, with absolutely nothing interesting in them.

39. ALDI Manvtii Romani Rvdimenta Grammatices Latinae Lingvae. *Venetiis Mense febr.* M. DI.   4to.

Extremely rare.

Aldus had long felt that he could not, notwithstanding his energy, do justice to all his work if he continued single-handed.   He collected around him a body of the most learned men of the age, whom he called *Aldi Neacademia.* On certain days they assembled in his house to discuss interesting literary points, to decide what authors should be published, and especially what manuscripts should be adopted as the text to be followed. These manuscripts he procured with infinite trouble and expense from all parts of Europe. About 1500 or 1501, Aldus married the daughter of Andrea Torresano, of Asola, also a Venetian printer, who, as I shall show later on, became his son-in-law's partner in 1508. In 1502, Aldus published sixteen works :

40. LVCANVS.—*Venetiis aprd Aldum mense Aprili. m. dii.* 8vo.
Collation : 132 leaves. It has not got the anchor.

41. IVLII Pollvcis Vocabvlarium.— *Venetiis apud Aldum mense Aprili. m. dii.* Folio.
Collation : 104 leaves, besides 8 leaves of indices. The title page follows the indices.
The *Editio princeps.*

42. THVCYDIDES *(Graece).* — *Venetiis in domo Aldi mense Maio. m. dii.* Folio.
Collation : 122 leaves.
Editio princeps. It is very rare.

43. LE Terze Rime di Dante.—*Venetiis in Aedib. Aldi. accuratissime. men. Aug. m. dii.* 8vo.

Collation: 252 leaves.

This is the first 8vo. edition of Dante.

44. SOPHOCLIS Tragaediæ *(sic)* septem cvm commentariis. *Graece.—Venetiis in Aldi Romani Academia mense Augusto. m. dii. Cautum et in hoc ut in caeteris, etc.* 8vo.

Collation: 196 leaves.

The title page is in Latin and Greek. This is the *Editio princeps.* Many people imagine that the fine old Aldine editions are merely literary curiosities: the following quotation from Brunck's preface to his edition of Sophocles, 1786, proves the value this learned editor set on the work done by Aldus:

" Primus edidit Aldus Manutius Romanus ex antiquis et probae notae codicibus. Praestantissima omnium haec editio est, quae majorem quam ceterae omnes auctoritatem habet, et plus quam quaevis alia fide digna est. Ex ea fere expressae sunt quaecumque dimidii seculi intervallo diversis in locis prodierunt. . . . Adr. Turnebus codicem a Demetrio Triclinio recensitum. . . . edidit. . . . ab ea discedere nefas duxerunt H. Stephanus et G. Canterus. . . . Verumtamen illa Triclinii interpolatio neutiquam digna erat, quæ sincero textui ab Aldo edito praeferretur: pravas lec·

C

tiones passim intrusit : maxime vero in canticis impudentissima audacia grassatus est. . . . Puritatem lectionis ex Aldina petendam esse semper fassi sunt viri doctiores. . . . Quapropter huic editioni Aldinam tamquam fundamentum substruxi : ad eam unice respexi, de reliquis nihil vel parum solicitus. Ubicumque ab ea disccssi, mutationis rationem in notis exposui. . . ."

45. CICERONIS Epistolæ familiares. —*Venetiis apud Aldum. m. d. ii. 8vo.*

An extremely rare volume, the existence of which is proved by its having formed part of the Pinelli Library (No. 3784).

46. LA Vita : e sito de Zichi : chiamati ciarcassi : historia notabile. (*di Giorgio Interiano Genovese*). — *Venetiis apud Aldum mense Octobri. m. dii.* 8vo.

Collation : 8 leaves.

Very rare.

47. HERODOTI libri novem. qvibvs Mvsarvm indita svnt nomina. *Graece.* —*Venetiis in domo Aldi mense Septembri. m. dii. et cum priuilegio ut in coeteris.* Folio.

Collation : 140 leaves.

Editio princeps et optima. One of the finest works printed by Aldus. It is rare, and happy is the possessor of one of the very few large paper copies that were printed !

48. VALERII Maximi Dictorvm et factorum memorabilivm libri novem.— *Venetiis in aedib. Aldi Romani Octobri mense. M. DII.* 8vo.

Collation : 216 leaves.

Editions of Valerius Maximus have been announced with the dates 1503, 1508, 1510, 1511, 1512, but no satisfactory proof has ever been furnished of their actual existence.

49. STATII Sylvarvm libri qvinqve Thebaidos libri dvodecim Achilleidos dvo. —*Venetiis in aedibvs Aldi. Mense Avgvsto. M. DII.* 8vo.

Collation : 292 leaves. ✗ 2S6

This volume should contain 40 leaves, sometimes placed at the beginning, sometimes at the end, with the following title-page in capitals :—

" Orthographia et flexvs dictionvm graecarvm omnivm apvd Stativm cvm accentib. et generib. ex variis vtrivsqve lingvae avtorib."

These 40 pages are dated " Mense Novembri. MDII." This has given rise to the belief of two editions of Statius in 1502.

50. OVIDII MetamorphoseΩn libri qvindecim. Ad Marinum Sannutum Epistola. qui apud græcos scripserint

μεταμορφώσεις.—*Venetiis in aedib. Aldi. mense Octobri. M. DII.* 8vo.

Collation: lxiv. and 204 leaves.

51. PVBLII Ovidii Nasonis Heroidvm Epistolae. Avli Sabini. Epistolae tres. P. O. N. Elegiarvm. Libri tres. Dc Arte amandi. Libri tres. De Remedio amoris, Libri duo. In Ibin. Liber unus. Ad Liviam Epistola de morte Drvsi. De Nvce. De Medicamine faciei.—*Venetiis in aedibvs Aldi Romani, mense Decembri. M. DII.* 8vo.

Collation: 202 leaves, leaf 120 being blank.

52. PVBLII Ovidii Nasonis, qvae hoc in libello continentvr. Fastorvm. Libri vi. De Tristibvs. Libri v.   De Ponto. Libri. iiii.—*Venetiis in Aldi Romani Academeia. mense Ianvario. M. DII.* 8vo.

Collation: 203 leaves.

The "De Tristibus" was only issued in 1503, but the "Fasti" bear the date of 1502.

This is one of the most precious of all the Aldine editions.

53. I. BAPTISTAE Egnatii Oratio in Lavdem Benedicti Prvnvli.—*Ex Academia Aldi Ro. M. DII. pri. Cal. Octob.* 8vo.

Very scarce.

54. STEPHANVS de Vrbibvs. *Graece.*
—*Venetiis apud Aldum Romanum mense
Ianuario. M. DII.* Folio.

Collation : 80 leaves.

Editio princeps. No anchor.

55. CATVLLVS. Tibvllvs. Propetivs.
(*sic*).—*Venetiis in aedibvs Aldi. mense
Ianvario. M. DII.* 8vo.

Collation: 44 leaves for Catullus; 36 for Tibullus;
70 for Propertius;—2 leaves, with colophon,
etc.

A fine copy on vellum is in the British Museum.

In the following year Aldus produced 10 works,
besides a catalogue, which I give entire in the
appendix to Vol. III.

56. QVE (*sic*) hoc volvmine continentvr.
Luciani opera. Icones Philostrati. Eius-
dem Heroica. Eiusdem uitæ Sophistarum.
Icones Iunioris Philostrati. Descriptiones
Callistrati.—*Venetiis in ædib. Aldi mense
Iunio. M. DIII.* Folio.

Collation: 572 pp., but only paged to 571, through
an error beginning p. 450.

A poor edition, from a literary point of view;
very inferior to the *Editio princeps,* Florence,
1496, folio.

57. AMMONII Hermei Commentaria

in librvm peri Hermenias. Margentini
(*lege Magentini*) Archiepiscopi Mitylen-
ensis in evndem enarratio. *Graece.—*
Venetiis apvd Aldvm mense Ivnio. M.
DIII. Folio.

Collation: 146 leaves.

In the preface to this work, Aldus assumed for
the first time the surname of *Pius*, after his friend
and protector, Albertus Pius, Prince of Carpi.

58. QVAE hoc in volvmine tractantvr.
Bessarionis Cardinalis Niceni & Patriarchæ
Constantinopolitani in calumniatorem
Platonis libri quatuor, etc.—*Venetiis in*
aedib. Aldi Romani, Ivlio mense M. D.
III. Folio.

Collation: 124 leaves.

A very rare book.

59. VLPIANI commentarioli in olynthiacas philippicas'q ; Demosthenis orationes
Enarrationes saneq necessariæ in tre-
decim orationes Demosthenis, (*Harpocra-*
tionis Lexicon decem Rhetorum.) *Graece.*
—Venetiis apud Aldum mense Octob. M.
D. III. Folio.

Collation: 179 leaves ;—1 blank leaf.

60. XENOPHONTIS omissa : quæ &
græca gesta appellantur. Georgii Gemisti :

qui & Pletho dicitur, etc. *Graece.—
Venetiis in Aldi Neacademia mense octobri
M. DIII.* Folio.

Collation : 156 leaves.

61. GEORGII Gemisti, qui & Pletho
dicitur, ex Diodori, & Plutarchi historiis
de iis, quæ post pugnam ad Mantineam
gesta sunt, per capita tractatio, etc.
*Graece. — Venetiis in Aldi Neacademia
mense octobri M. D. III.* Folio.

Regarding this book Renouard writes as follows :

" Ce volume est une portion du précédent. Fr.
Asulanus, imprimant en 1525 Xénophon complet,
et ayant encore des exemplaires de son recueil de
1503, en ôta la première partie, qui ne contenait
qu'une petite portion de Xénophon, et fit un
nouveau titre, avec une courte préface au verso de
ce titre, dans laquelle il expliquait qu'il s'était
arrangé ainsi pour qu'on pût acquérir ce volume
et le joindre au Xénophon de 1525, sans avoir
cependant rien de répété.

" Ce titre et cette préface ont donc été imprimés
après l'année 1525, époque de la publication du
Xénophon entier. J'en ai un exemplaire réuni,
dans son ancienne reliure, avec l'édition d'Ulpien,
de 1527 ; et la confrontation de la dernière page
de cet Ulpien avec le titre de Gemistius, m'a con-
vaincu que ce titre a été fait en 1527, en même
temps que l'edition d'Ulpien, précisément avec les
mêmes caractères et autres pièces d'imprimerie."

62. FLORILEGIVM diversorvm epi-

grammatvm in septem libros.   *Graece.—*
Venetiis in ædibus Aldi mense Nouembri.
M. DIII.   8vo.

Collation : 290 leaves.

This is the rarest and handsomest of the three
editions issued by the Aldine press.   Some copies
were printed on vellum : one was in Dr Askew's
library.

63. EVRIPIDIS tragoediæ septende-
cim, ex quib. quædam habent commentaria, etc.—*Venetiis apvd Aldvm mense*
febrvario.   *M. D. III.*   2 vol.   8vo.

Collation : Vol. I., 268 leaves—Vol. II., 190
leaves.

Edito princeps.   It contains · 18 tragedies, although only 17 are mentioned on the title-page,
Hercules Furens having been added at the end of
Vol. II.   In the preface Aldus mentions that he
usually printed 1000 copies of his 8vo. editions,
although in the preface to the Catullus of 1502 he
mentions having printed 3000 copies of that book.
This book is rare.   A vellum copy is in the British
Museum.

64. QVAE hoc in libro continentvr.
Origenis in Genesim Homiliæ. 16. Eiusdem in Exodum Homiliæ. 13. Eiusdem
in Leuiticum Homiliæ. 16. Eiusdem. in

Numeros Homiliæ. 28. Eiusdem in Iesum
Naue Homiliæ. 26. Eiusdem in Librum
Iudicum Homiliæ. 8. (*Latine*) Diuo Hier-
onymo interprete.—*Ven. in aedib. Aldi.
Ro. mense feb. M. D. III.* Folio.

Collation : vi and 182 leaves.

In 1504 Aldus produced six works :

65. SCIPIONIS Carteromachi Pistori-
ensis Oratio de Lavdibvs literarvm graecarvm Venetiis habita mense Ianvario.
M. D. IIII.—*Venetiis ex Aldi Neacademia
mense Maio. M. D. III.* 8vo.

Collation : 15 leaves ;—1 blank leaf.
Very rare.

66. IOANNIS grammatici in Posteriora
resolutoria Aristotelis Comentaria. *Graece.
—Venetiis apud Aldum mense Martio.
M. DIIII.* Folio.

Collation : 295 pp. ; numbered on both sides ;—
12 unnumbered leaves.

This is the first vol. in which Aldus numbered
each page.

67. HABENTVR hoc Volvmine haec
Theodoro Gaza interprete.

Aristotelis de natura animalium. lib. ix.,
etc. *Latine.—Venetiis mense Martio. M.
D. IIII.* Folio. -

Collation: xxviii and 274 leaves.

68. GREGORII Nazanzeni Carmina, cum versione latina.—*Venetiis ex Aldi Academia mense Iunio.* M. DIII. 4to.

Collation: 232 leaves.

This forms the 3rd vol. of the collection of Christian poets.

69. HOMERI Opera omnia, cum vita ejus ex Herodoto, Dione et Plutarcho. *Graece.—2 calend. nouemb. 1504.* 2 vols. 8vo.

Collation: Iliad, 277 leaves;—1 blank leaf;—
    Odyssey, 250 leaves ;—Life of Homer, 56
    leaves.

This edition has often been announced as without a date, probably because the date only appears in the preface to the Odyssey. Copies were printed on vellum.

70. DEMOSTHENIS orationes duæ & sexaginta. Libanii sophistæ in eas ipsas orationes argumenta. Vita Demosthenis per Libanium. Eiusdem uita per Plutarchum. *Graece.—Venetiis in ædib. Aldi. mense Nouem.* M. D. IIII. Folio.

Collation: part i., xxviii. and 320 pp. ; part ii.,
    286 pp.;—6 unnumbered pages ;—1 blank leaf.

Of this book there are two editions ; the first,

which is the rarest and the handsomest, may be recognised by the Aldine Anchor having the name of the printer thus

ALDVS 🛟 MA. RO.

Whilst the second has the name divided thus—

AL   DVS.

It appears that in 1513 Aldus, when printing his Greek orators being out of his Demosthenes of 1504, reprinted it, but with the same date of 1504. The second edition is the best from a literary point of view. It appears from the preface that Aldus printed a very small number of copies; why, we have no means of ascertaining.

71. CIMBRIACI poetæ Encomiastica ad Federicum Imp. et Maximilianum Regem Roman.—*Venetiis, apud Aldum m. d. iiii.* 8vo.

This is the first edition of these little poems which were edited by Giovanni da Camerino, professor of Theology at Vienna.

Seven works were issued in 1505:

72. GLI Asolani di Messer Pietro Bembo.—*Impressi in Venetiis nelle Case d'Aldo Romano nel anno m. dv. del mese di Marzo.* 4to.

Collation : 96 leaves;—1 leaf marked N containing errata ;—1 blank leaf. In some copies page 2 of sheet A i is blank and sheet A ii is wanting. It appears that the dedication was addressed to Lucrezia Borgia, daughter of Pope Alexander vi., and wife at that time of Alphonso d'Este, Duke of Ferrara. Whilst the work was being printed, disputes arose between Alphonso and Julius ii., and Aldus, who was devoted to the Holy See, thought it best to suppress the dedication. This necessitated the reprinting of the title page and the suppression of sheet marked A ii, on which the dedication was being printed. Copies with the dedication are of course extremely rare.

73. I. AVRELIVS Avgvrellvs. — *Venetiis in aedibvs Aldi mense Aprili. m. d. v.* 8vo.

Collation : 128 leaves.

Rare.

74. HORAE in lavdem beatiss. Virginis secundum consuetudinem Romanæ curiæ. Septem Psalmi pœnitentiales cum litaniis, & orationibus. Sacrificivm in laudem Sanctiss. Virginis. *Graece.— Venetiis apud Aldum. mense Iulio. m. d. v.* 32mo.

Collation : 160 leaves.

An edition announced by Unger as being without a date, was probably the above with leaf 160

wanting.   This might easily occur, as at the end
of leaf 159 is the word

ΤΕΛΟΣ.

75. PONTANI   opera. — *Venetiis   in
ædibus Aldi Ro. mense augusto M. d. v.*
8vo.

Collation : 241 leaves.

76. ADRIANI Cardinalis S. Chryso-
goni ad Ascanium Cardinalem Venatio.—
Venetiis apud Aldum mense Sept. M. d. v.
8vo.

Collation : 8 leaves—*no title page.*
It is very rare.

77. VITA, et Fabellæ Aesopi cum
interpretatione latina, &c.—*Venetiis apud
Aldum mense Octobri. m. d. v.* Sm. folio.

Collation: 150 leaves in all.
A beautiful and rare edition.

78. VERGILIVS.—*Venetiis m. d. v.
mense Decembri.* 8vo.

Collation : viii and 304 leaves;—1 leaf with
anchor.
As rare as the edition of 1501.

In 1506, the war which raged in Italy caused
Aldus to leave Venice, and his works were therefore closed.   He lost heavily through the war, and

when he returned to Venice in 1507, he found himself poorer than when he had left it. He began to work, but found himself crippled by want of means. He only managed to produce one work,

79. HECVBA, et Iphigenia in Aulide Euripidis tragœdiæ in latinum tralatæ Erasmo Roterodamo interprete, etc.— *Venetiis in aedibvs Aldi mense Decembri. M. dvii.* 8vo.

Collation : 80 leaves.

A rare and little known volume.

In 1508, Andrea Torresano, or, as he is better known, Andrea d'Asola, entered into partnership with him, and his capital enabled Aldus to push ahead with his masterpieces. The first bearing this date is

80. ALDI Manvtii Romani Institvtionvm Grammaticarvm libri quatvor.— *Venetiis apud Aldvm Aprili mense m. d. viii.* 4to.

Collation : 192 leaves.

It seems that this work must have been published just before Andrea d' Asola joined Aldus, as all works published by them jointly bear the imprint, "*In Aedibus Aldi.*"

81. ERASMI Roterodami Adagiorum

Chiliades tres, ac centuriæ fere totidem.
—*Venetiis in Aedibus Aldi. Mense Sept. m.
dviii.* Folio.

Collation : 249 leaves—two indices.

Aldus states in his preface, that he put aside all
other work in order to publish this useful and
learned book.

82. C. PLINII Secvndi Novocomensis
epistolarum libri Decem, in quibus multæ
habentur epistolæ non ante impressæ, &c.
— *Venetiis in Aedib. Aldi, et Andreæ Asulani
Soceri. Mense Nouembri. m. d. viii.* 8vo.

Collation : xxiv. and 525 pages—1 leaf with
anchor.

83. RHETORES graeci.   1508, 1509.
—*Venetiis in ædib. Aldi. mense Nouembris.
m. d viii.* Folio.

Collation : Vol. I., xvi and 734 pages ;—12 pages
of tables ;—leaf with register and colophon.
Vol. II., xxviii and 417 pages ;—1 leaf with
anchor.

A very rare work.   ᴀ

In March and April, 1509, Aldus published
three works :

84. PLVTARCHI Opvscvla. lxxxxii
Graece.—*Venetiis, in ædibus Aldi &* An-
dreæ Asulani Soceri. Mense Martio. m. dix.
Folio.

Collation: xxxii and 1050 pages;—1 leaf with anchor.

Editio princeps. A copy on vellum is in the Bibliothèque Nationale, bound in two volumes, bearing the arms of Henri II.

85. Q. HORATII Flacci poemata.— *Venetiis apvd Aldvm Romanvm mense Martio. m. d. ix.* 8vo.

Collation: xlviii and 310 pages :—1 blank leaf.

This edition is more correct, and almost as rare as that of 1501.

86. C. CRISPI Sallvstii de Conivratione Catilinae. Eivsdem de Bello Ivgvrthino. Eiusdem oratio contra. M. T. Ciceronem. M. T. Ciceronis oratio contra. C. Crispum Sallustium. Eiusdem orationes quatuor contra Lucium Catilinam. Porcii Latronis declamatio contra Lucium Catilinam Orationes quædam ex libris historiarum. C. Crispi Sallustii.— *Venetiis in Aedibus Aldi, et Andreæ Asulani soceri Mense Aprili. mdix.* 8vo.

Collation: xvi and 279 pages.

War again forced Aldus to close his establishment. During the latter part of 1509, and the whole of the years 1510 and 1511, no book was published by him, although several have been announced by bibliographers, which will be found mentioned under "Imaginary Editions," in Vol. iii. In 1512, the year his third son, Paulus Manutius, was born, he resumed work, and three works bear that date :

87. CONSTANTINI Lascaris Byzantini de octo partibus orationis, etc.—*Venetiis apud Aldum mense octobri. m. d. xii.* 4to.

Collation: 270 leaves ;—20 leaves of appendix.

88. EROTEMATA Chrysoloræ. De anomalis uerbis. De formatione temporum ex libro Chalcondylæ. Quartus Gazæ de Constructione. De Encliticis. Sententiæ monostichi ex uarijs poetis. *Graece.— Venetiis in ædib Aldi m. d. xii.* 8vo.

Collation: 296 pages.   Rare.

89. M. T. C. EPISTOLAE familiares accvrativs recognitae. M. D. XII. Index etiam ad inueniendum, quota nam charta habeantur singulæ quæq; epistolæ.— *Venetiis apvd Aldvm et Andream socervm.* 8vo.

Collation: 275 leaves.

As rare as the edition of 1502.

The year 1513 was a busy one: no less than ten works issuing from the press, viz.:

90. PINDARI. Olympia, etc. *Graece.—*

D

Venetijs* in ædib. Aldi, et Andreæ Asulani Soceri, Mense Ianuario M. d. xiii.   8vo.

Collation: xvi and 374 pages ;—1 blank leaf.

Editio princeps of all the authors contained in it, except Callimachus.   Rare.

91. STROZII poetæ Pater et Filivs. —*M. dxiii.*   8vo.

Collation: viii and 252 leaves.

92. HABENTVR hoc Volvmine Haec Theodoro Gaza interprete.   Aristotelis de natura animalium lib. ix., etc.   *Latine.-- Februario M. d. xiii.*   Folio.

Collation: xii and 273 leaves ;—1 leaf with the anchor ;—16 leaves of vocabularies.

The imprint will be found on folio 108.

93. Hoc volvmine continentvr haec. Commentariorum de bello Gallico, etc.— *M. d. xiii. Mense Aprili.*   8vo.

Collation: xx and 296 leaves.

The date will be found on page 264.

94. RHETORUM graecorum Orationes.   *Graece.—Maii m. d. xiii.*   Folio.

Collation: Part i., 2 leaves, followed by pages

---

* As the imprint of all editions from the Aldine press till 1529 bear the words "Venetiis in ædibus Aldi et Andreæ Soceri," or "Venitiis in ædibus Aldi et Andreæ Asulani Soceri," I henceforth omit these words in all imprints up to that date.

3 to 197 ;—1 blank leaf.   Part ii., 163 pages ;
the last numbered 162 in error.   Part iii., 267
pages mostly numbered wrong.

An invaluable work.

95. M. T. CICERONIS epistolarum
ad Atticum, etc.—*Ivnio m. dxiii.*   8vo.

Collation : xvi and 331 leaves.

96. OMNIA Platonis opera.   *Graece.*
Septembri. m. d. xiii   Folio.

Collation : Part I., xxx and 502 pages.   Part II.,
439 pages.   Very rare.'

97. ALEXANDRI Aphrodisiei in
Topica Aristotelis, Commentarii.   *Graece.*
—*Septembri. m. d. xiii.*   Folio.

Collation : iv and 279 pages (numbered from 3 to
281);—1 leaf with the anchor.

98. In hoc volvmine habentvr haec
(*Nicolai Perotti Sypontini*).

Cornvcopiae, siue linguæ latinæ commentarij diligentissime recogniti, etc.—
Novembri. m. d. xiii.   Folio.

Collation : clviii and 718 pages, with 1 blank
leaf after the preliminary matter ;—1 leaf with
anchor.

99. PONTANI (*Joannis Joviani*) opera.
—*m. d. xiii.*   8vo.

Collation : 255 leaves ;—1 leaf with anchor.

A more correct edition than that of 1505.

In 1514, Aldus gave the world eleven books :

100. SVIDA.—*Feb. m. v. xiiii.*

Collation : 391 leaves.

The title page is entirely in Greek.

101. RHETORICORUM ad C. Herennium lib. iiii., etc.—*Martio m. d. xiiii.* 8vo.

Collation : ' vi and 245 leaves ;—3 leaves for *errata* and anchor.

102. LIBRI de Re rvstica.—*Maio m. d. xiiii.* 4to.

Collation : xxxiv and 308 leaves.

103. HESYCHII Dictionarium. *Graece.* —*Augusto m. d. xiiii.* Folio.

Collation : 196 leaves ;—1 leaf with anchor.

104. ATHENAEVS. *Graece.*—*Avgvsto. m d xiiii.* _ Folio.

Collation : xxxviii and 294 pages, with a blank leaf after the preliminary matter ;—1 leaf with anchor.

Editio princeps. Very rare.

105. M. F. QVINTILIANVS. — *Avgvsto m. d. xiiii.* 4to.

Collation : iv and 230 leaves

106. IL PETRARCHA.—*M. d. xiiii. Agosto.* 8vo.

Collation : 184 leaves ;—24 leaves of tables, verses, &c.

Considered the "Editio Optima Aldina" by Ludovicus Castelvetro and other Italian writers.

*(See that folio 64 is **not** wanting. Being an attack on Rome, it is often torn out.)*

107. ARCADIA del Sannazaro.—*M. d. xiiii. Settembre.* 8vo.

Collation: 89 leaves ;—1 leaf with anchor.

108. VIRGILIVS.—*M. d. xiiii. Octobri.* 8vo.

Collation : 224 leaves.

109. VALERIVS Maximvs.—*Octobri. m. d. xiiii.* 8vo.

Collation : 216 leaves.

110. ALDI Pii Manvtii Institvtionvm Grammaticarvm libri qvatuor.—*Decembri. m. d. xiiii.* 4to.

Collation: 210 leaves.

Under the date of 1515, we find ten works :

111. LVCRETIVS.—*Ianvario. m. d. xv.* 8vo.

Collation: viii and 125 leaves ;—2 leaves for *errata* and anchor.

Much more correct than the edition of 1500.

112. CATVLLVS Tibvllvs Propertivs. —*Martio. m. d. xv.* 8vo.

Collation : 148 leaves ;—2 leaves for register and anchor.

113. L. CŒLII Lactantii Firmiani diuinarum institutionum Libri septem.— *Aprili. m. d. xv.* 8vo.

Collation : 428 leaves in all.

114. P. OUIDII Nasonis uita ex ipsius libris excerpta. Heroidum Epistolæ Amorum libri iii. De arte amandi libri iii. De remedio amoris libri ii. De medicamine faciei. Nux Somnium,— *Maio. m. d. xv.* 8vo.

Collation : xvi and 182 leaves.

115. GLI Asolani di Messer Pietro Bembo.—*M. d. xv. Maggio.* 8vo.

Collation : 130 leaves.

116. LVCANVS.—*Ivlio. m. d. xv.* 8vo.

Collation : 132 leaves.

117. ERASMI Roterodami Opvscvlvm, cvi titvlvs est Moria, id est Stvltitia, qvae pro concione loqvitvr.—*Avgvsto. m. d. xv.* 8vo.

Collation : iv and 48 leaves.

118. DANTE col-sito, et forma dell' Inferno tratta dalla istessa descrittione del Poeta.—*M. d. xv. Agosto.* 8vo.

Collation : 248 leaves.

119. AVLI Gellii Noctivm Atticarvm libri undeviginti.—*Septembri. m. d. xv.* 8vo.

Collation : xxxii and 340 leaves.

120. ALDI Manvtii Romani grammaticae institvtiones graecae. — *Novembri m. d. xv.* 4to.

Collation: 136 leaves.

The preface, addressed to Jean Grolier, so well known to lovers of fine bindings, is extremely curious. The book is extremely rare.

Two other works were published by Aldus without a date—viz.:

121. QVINTI Calabri Derelictorvm ab Homero libri quatvordecim. *Grœce.* 8vo. And

122. CONSTANTINI Lascaris Byzantini de octo partibus orationis, etc.,— *Venetiis apud Aldum.* 4to.

The former has 172 leaves, the latter 298.

The *Calaber* is generally assigned to 1521, but I believe 1505 to be more correct, whilst the Lascaris must have appeared between 1498 and 1503.

In the month of April of this year Aldus closed his laborious career, dying at the age of 70. He left four children—Manutio de, Manutii, who became priest and lived at Asola, where he was often visited by his brother Paulus; Antonio, who cultivated literature, and was certainly a bookseller at Bologna, if not a printer (see under the year 1556); Paulus Manutius, born in 1512, who afterwards carried on his father's business; and a daughter, whose name is unknown, but who married a certain Julio Catone, of Mantua.

It is difficult to picture to ourselves the passion with which Aldus reproduced the master-pieces of ancient literature, and it would seem impossible that one man should have been able to carry on simultaneously the laborious occupations of a printer, editor, and author, besides delivering lectures on a variety of subjects to the youth of Venice. Such men are rare in our day, and though I know an instance or two, the men themselves, in most cases, pass unnoticed by the crowd, and are often looked down upon by the vulgar. Happily for Aldus, such has not been the case with him. The names of the Estiennes, the Plantins, and especially of the Elzeviers and of Aldus and his son, will live as long as men study the gems of antiquity! Honour to those who have rescued from the obliterating dust of ages those marvellous productions of Greece and of Rome, which, had it not been for their days of labour and nights of toilsome research, had probably, long ere now, been lost to us for ever !

END OF VOL. I.

The Aldine Press.

Bibliotheca Curiosa.

A BIBLIOGRAPHICAL SKETCH

OF

THE ALDINE PRESS
AT VENICE,

FORMING

A CATALOGUE

*Of all Works issued by Aldus and his successors,
from 1494 to 1597, and a list of all known
Forgeries or Imitations,*

TRANSLATED AND ABRIDGED FROM

ANT. AUG. RENOUARD'S

" Annales de L'Imprimerie des Aldes,"

AND

REVISED AND CORRECTED

BY

EDMUND GOLDSMID, F.R.H.S., F.S.A. (Scot.)

IN THREE VOLUMES.
VOL. II.
ANDREA D'ASOLA & PAULUS MANUTIUS

PRIVATELY PRINTED, EDINBURGH.

—

1887.

THE ALDINE PRESS.

ANDREA D'ASOLA AND HIS SONS.

FTER the death of Aldus, his children being still quite young, his father-in-law, Andrea d'Asola, undertook the management of the printing establish-ment, assisted by his two sons, Francesco and Frederick. From 1515 to 1529 edition followed edition in rapid succession, and if, from a literary point of view, the works which issued from the Aldine Press during these fourteen years are inferior as a rule to those of Aldus, or of Paul Manutius, they are at any rate beautifully printed, most of them rare, and much sought after. One mistake Andrea Torresano made: instead of

gathering round him men whose learning might
have assisted him in the difficult task which had
now fallen to his share, either from false economy
or literary presumption, he endeavoured to do the
whole of the editing assisted only by his sons.

All the works, with few exceptions, printed
during the regency, if we may so call it, of Andrea
d'Asola bear the imprint: *In Aedibus Aldi et
Andreae Asulani Soceri,* and I shall therefore
omit this imprint, save where any difference
appears in the formula.

In 1516 eleven works appeared :

123. QVAE in hoc volvmine continentvr.
Annotationes in omnia Ouidij opera,
etc.   Febrvario M.D. XVI.   8vo.

Collation: xlviii and 204 leaves.

124. CLA. PTOLEMAEI inerrantivm
Stellarum significationes per Nicolaum
Leonicum è græco translatæ, etc.   Ian-
vario M.D. XVI.   8vo.

Collation: xxii and 227 leaves ; 1 leaf with anchor.

This edition is nearly as rare as the first, and is
superior to it as regards purity of text.   Some
vellum copies are known.

125. LUDOVICI Cœlii Rhodigini Lec-
tionum antiquarum libri sexdecim.   Febrvario M.D. XVI.   Folio.

Collation: 862 pages;—3 unnumbered leaves.

Before the text are 40 leaves of tables, &c., and the first page does not bear the title of the book, but a kind of advertisement printed in red capitals.

126. GREGORII. Nazanzeni Theologi Orationes lectissimae xvi. *Graece.* Aprili. M.D. XVI. 8vo.

Collation: viii and 311 leaves;—1 leaf with anchor.

127. LVCIANI Opvscvla Erasmo Rotero-damo interprete. Toxaris, siue de Amicitia. Alexander, qui & Pseudomantis. Gallus, siue Somnium Timon, seu Misanthropus. Tyrannicida, seu pro tyrannicida. De-clamatio Erasmi contra tyrannicidam. De ijs, qui mercede conducti degunt. Et quædam eiusdem alia Eiusdem Luciani Thoma Moro Interprete, Cynicus Menip-pus, seu Necromantia Philopseudes, seu incredulus. Tyrannicida da Declamatio Mori de eodem. Maio M.D. XVI. 8vo.

Collation: 238 leaves.

This volume is extremely rare.

128. PAVSANIAS. *Graece.* Ivlio. M.D XVI. Folio.

Collation: iv and 282 pages;—1 leaf with anchor.

129. IOANNIS Baptistæ Egnatij Veneti de Cæsaribus libri III à Dictatore Cæsare ad Constantinum Palæologum, hinc à Carolo Magno ad Maximilianum Cæsarem. Eiusdem in Spartiani, Lampridijq; uitas, & reliquorum annotationes. Neruæ & Traiani atq; Adriani principum uitæ ex Dione, Georgio Merula interprete. Aelius Spartianus Iulius Capitolinus Lampridius Flauius Vopiscus Trebellius Pollio Vulcatius Gallicanus ab eodem Egnatio castigati. Addita in calce Heliogabali principis ad meretrices elegantissima oratio non ante impressa. Ivlio. M.D. XVI. 8vo.

Collation: Part i., 108 leaves; Part ii., 296 leaves.

130. C. SUETONIJ Tranquili XII Cæsares. Sexti Aurelij Victoris à D. Cæsare Augusto usq; ad Theodosium excerpta. Eutropij de gestis Romanorum. Lib. x. Pauli Diaconi libri VIII ad Eutropij historiam additi. Augusto. M.D XVI. 8vo.

Collation: xxxii and 320 leaves.

Rare, and generally found in poor condition.

131. BESSARIONIS Cardinalis Niceni, & Patriarchæ Constantinopolitani in calumniatorem Platonis libri quatuor, etc. *Latine.* Septembri. M.D. XVI. Folio.

Collation: Part i., viii and 116 leaves.—Part ii., 56 leaves.

This edition is not rare.

132. STRABO de Sitv orbis. *Graece.* Novembri. M.D. XVI. Folio.

Collation: xxviii and 366 pages, the last being wrongly numbered 348 ;—1 leaf with anchor.

Editio princeps.

133. IAMBLICHVS de mysteriis Ægyptiorum, Chaldæorum, Assyriorum, etc. *Latine.* Novembri. M.D. XVI. Folio.

Collation: 175 leaves, the last wrongly numbered 177.

Ten works bear the date of 1517 :

134. HOMERI opera omnia, cūm vita ejus ex Herodoto, Dione et Plutarcho. *Graece.* Ivnio M.D. XVII. 8vo.

Collation: Illiad, 277 leaves ;—1 blank leaf ;— Odyssey, 252 leaves ; Life of Homer, 56 leaves.

Rarer than the edition of 1504, and far more correct.

135. M. T. Cic. Officiorvm Libri III. Cato maior, sive de Senectvte. Laelivs, sive de Amicitia. Somnivm Scipionis, ex VI. de Rep. excerptvm. Ivnio. M.D. XVII. 8vo.

The only copy known was sold in London in 1792 ; at least Renouard states the fact, and adds that it was printed on vellum.

136. SCENECAE *(sic)* Tragoediae. Octobri. M.D. XVII.   8vo.

Collation : iv and 212 leaves.

Vellum copies are known.

137. TERENTIVS. Novembri. M.D. XVII.   8vo.

This edition is one of the rarest of the whole Aldine series.

138. EROTEMATA Chrysoloræ. De anomalis uerbis. De formatione temporum ex libro Chalcondylæ. Quartus Gazæ de Constructione. De Encleticis. Sententiæ monostichi ex uarijs poetis. Cato. Erotemata Guarini. *Graece.* Novembri. M.D. XVII.   8vo.

Collation: 415 pages.

139. AVSONIVS. Novembri. M.D. XVII.   8vo.

Collation: 108 leaves.

140. MUSÆI opusculum de Herone & Leandro. *(Graece et Latine)* Orphei argonautica. Eiusdem hymni. Orpheus de lapidibus. *Graece.* Novembri. M.D. XVII. 8vo.

Collation : 80 leaves.

141. OPPIANI de piscibus libri v.

Eiusdem de uenatione libri IIII. Oppiani
de piscibus Laurentio Lippio interprete
libri V.   Decembri. M.D. XVII.   8vo.

Collation: 169 leaves.

142. MARTIALIS.   Decembri. M.D.
XVII.   8vo.

Collation: 192 leaves.

143. DIVERSORVM vetervm poetarvm
in Priapvm Lvsus.   Decembri. M.D. XVII.
8vo.

Collation: 80 leaves, the last wrongly numbered
90.

A beautiful and very rare edition.   There is a
large-paper copy in the British Museum.

In 1518, Torresano issued 10 works :

144. IOANNIS Ioviani Pontani amorum
libri II., etc.   Febrvario. M. D. XVIII.   8vo.

Collation: 172 leaves.

145.   AESCHYLI   tragoediæ   sex.
Graece.   Febrvario. M D XVIII.   8vo.

Collation: 114 leaves.

Editio princeps.   Very incomplete.

146. SACRAE Scriptvrae veteris, novae'
qve omnia.   *Graece.*   Febrvario M D XVIII.
Folio.

Collation: iv and 454 leaves.

Very rare.

147. C. PLINII Secvndi Novocomensis Epistolarum libri x., etc. Ivnio. M. D. XVIII. 8vo.

Collation : xxviii and 526 leaves.

148. DIOSCORIDES. (*Graece.*) Ivnio. M. D. XVIII.   4to.

Collation : xii and 244 leaves.

149. IOANNIS Ioviani Pontani opera omnia solvta oratione composita.   Iunio. M. D. XVIII.   4to.

Collation : iv and 327 leaves.

The first of the three volumes of the works of Pontanus.   The other two appeared in 1519.

150. ARTEMIDORI De somniorum interpretatione Libri Quinq ;. De Insomniis, Quod Synesii Cuiusdam nomine circumfertur. *Graece.*   Avgvsto M. D. XVIII. 8vo.

Collation : 164 leaves.

Editio princeps.   Very rare.

151. (*Desiderii Erasmi opuscula*) PACIS Qverela.   De regno administrando.   Institutio Principis Christiani.   Panegyricus ad Philippum & carmen.   Item ex Plvtarcho. De discrimine adulatoris & amici.   De utilitate capienda ex inimicis.   De doctrina Principum.   Principi   cum   philosopho

semper esse disputandum. Item. Declamatio super puero mortuo. Septembri.
M. D. XVIII. 8vo.

Collation : 224 leaves.

Very rare.

152. POMPONIVS Mela. Ivlivs Soli-
nvs. Itinerarivm Antonini Avg. Vibivs
Seqvester. P. Victor de regionibus urbis
Romæ. Dionysius Afer de Situ orbis
Prisciano interprete. Octobri M. D. XVIII.
8vo.

Collation : 236 leaves.

153. EX XIIII. T. Livii Decadibus
Prima, Tertia, Qvarta, in qua præter fragmenta iii, & x libri, quæ in Germania
nuper reperta, hic etiam continentur,
multa adulterina expunximus, multa uera
recepimus, quæ in alijs non habentur.
Epitome singulorum librorum xiiii Decadum. Historia omnium xiiii Decadum
in compendium redacta ab L. Floro.
Polibij lib. v de rebus Romanis latinitate
donati à Nicolao Perotto. Index copiosis-
simus rerum omnium memorabilium.
Decembri. M. D. XVIII. 8vo.

Collation : lxviii and 373 leaves.

This is the first volume of Livy, 8vo ; the others

appeared in 1519, 1521, and 1533. Renouard says :—

"Le titre ci-dessus rapporté prouve que le Florus, in-8vo, sans date, et le Polybe latin de 1521, annoncés par plusieurs comme des éditions distinctes et complètes en elles-mêmes, font nécessairement partie de cette édition de Tite-Live, et ne sont, séparées, que des fragments imparfaits. Il paraît qu'on en aura tiré un nombre en sus, pour être vendu à part ; car on en trouve assez fréquemment, et sur-tout du Florus.

Thirteen works bear the date of 1519 :

154. STATII Sylvarvm libri v, etc. Ianvario. M. D. XIX. 8vo.

Collation : 296 leaves.

155. M. T. CICERONIS Orationvm Volvmen primvm. Ianvario. M. D. XVIIII. 8vo.

Collation : xii and 308 leaves.

156. M. T. CICERONIS Orationvm Volvmen secvndvm. Maii M D XIX. 8vo.

Collation : vii and 281 leaves.

157. M. T. CICERONIS Orationvm Volvmen tertivm. Avgvsto. M. D. XIX. 8vo.

Collation : vi and 278 leaves.

A complete set of the first Aldine edition of Cicero is an extraordinary rarity. It consists of

1. Libri Oratorii, 4to, 1514.
2. Orationes, 3 vols., 8vo, 1518-19.

3. Epist. ad Atticum, 8vo, 1513.
4. Epist. ad Familiares, 8vo, 1502 or 1512.
5. Opera philosophica, 2 vols., 8vo, 1523.
6. De Officiis, 8vo, 1517 or 1519.

158. M. T. CIC. Officiorvm. Lib. iii. Cato Maior, sive de Senectvte. Laelivs, sive de Amicitia. Somnivm Scipionis ex vi. de Rep. excerptvm. Febrvario. M. D. XIX. 8vo.

Collation : viii and 160 leaves.

159. TITI Livii Patavini Decas tertia. Febrvario. M. D. XIX. 8vo.

Collation : 356 leaves ;—48 leaves of index.

Second vol. of Livy.

160. IOANNIS Ioviani Pontani. De Aspiratione Libri duo. Charon Dialogus. Antonivs Dialogus. Activs Dialogus. Aegidivs Dialogus. Asinvs Dialogus. De Sermone Libri Sex. Beli, qvod Ferdinandvs Senior Neapolitanvs Rex cvm Ioanne Andeganiensivm *(sic)* dvce gessit, libri sex. Aprili. M. D. XIX. 4to.

Collation : 318 leaves.

161. CENTVM Ptolemaei Sententiae ad Syrvm fratrem à Pontano è graeco in latinvm tralatae, atqve expositae. Eivsdem Pontani libri xiiii. de Reb. coelestibvs. Liber etiam de Lvna imperfectvs. Sep· temb. M. D. XIX.· 4to.

Collation: 320 leaves.

162. NERVAE & Traiani, atq; Adriani Cæsarum uitæ ex Dione, etc. Avgvsto. M. D. XIX. 8vo.

Collation: 424 leaves.

163. PLVTARCHI qvae vocantur Parallela. Hoc est Vitae illvstrivm virorvm graeci nominis ac latini, provt qvaeqve alteri convenire videbatvr, digestae. *Graece.* Avgvste. M. D. XIX. Folio.

Collation: iv and 346 leaves.

It is said there are two editions under this date. I cannot myself assert that I have met with any satisfactory proof of this, though Renouard seems convinced of the fact.

164. Q. HORATII Flacci Poemata omnia. Centimetrum Marij Seruij. Annotationes Aldi Manutij Romani in Horatium. Ratio mensuum, quibus Odæ eiusdem Poëtæ tenentur eodem Aldo authore. Nicolai Peroti libellus eiusdem argumenti. Novembri. M. D. XIX. 8vo.

Collation: viii and 192 leaves.

165. COMMENTARIORUM de bello Gailico libri viii., etc. Novemb. M. D. XIX. 8vo.

Collation: xvi and 296 leaves.

A reprint of the edition of 1513.

We only meet with 6 works in 1520, viz.:

166. QVINTVS CVRTIVS. Ivlio.
M. D. XX. 8vo.
Collation: viii and 172 leaves.
Rare.

167. ALEXANDRI aphrodisiensis, in priora analytica Aristotelis, commentaria. *Graece. — Venetiis, apud Aldum et Andream Asulanum. 1520. Leonardo Lauredano principe, &c.* Folio.
Collation: 142 leaves.

168. ALEXANDRI Aphrodisiensis, in Sophisticos Aristotelis Elenchos, Commentaria. *Graece.* Octobri. M. D. XX. Folio.
Collation: 66 leaves.

169. TITI Livii Patavini Decas qvarta. Novembri. M. D. XX. 8vo.
Collation: xii and 296 leaves; — 44 leaves of Index.

170. EX XIIII. T. Livii Decadibvs Prima Tertia Qvarta, etc. Folio.
Collation: 394 leaves.
Very rare.

171. ERASMI Roterodami Adagiorvm Chiliades qvatvor, Centuriaeqve totidem. Qvibvs etiam qvinta additvr imperfecta. Septembri. M. D. XX. Folio.
Collation: xxvi and 304 leaves.

B

A beautiful and very rare edition.

In 1521, fourteen works saw the light :

172. M. FABII Qvintiliani Institutionum Oratoriarum libri xii diligentius recogniti. Ianvario. M. D. XXI. 4to.

Collation : iv and 230 leaves.

173. M. T. CICERONIS. Epistolarvm ad Atticvm, ad Brvtvm, ad Qvintvm fratrem, libri xx. nvper exacta recogniti cura. M. D. XXI. Latina interpretatio eorum, quæ græce scripta sunt, &c. Ianvario. M. D. XXI. 8vo.

Collation : vi and 331 leaves.

174. C. CRISPI Sallvstii de Conivratione Catilinae. Eiusdem de bello Iugurthino, etc. Ianvario M. D. XXI. 8vo.

Collation : viii and 144 leaves.

A better edition than that of 1509.

175. FLORILEGIVM diversorvm Epigrammatvm in septem libros. Solerti nuper repurgatum cura. M. D. XXI. *Graece.* Ianvario. M. D. XXI. 8vo.

Collation : 290 leaves.

176. TITI Livii Patavini librorvm Epitomae. Lvcivs Florvs. Martio. M. D. XXI. 8vo.

Collation : Livy, 56 leaves ;—·Florus, 68 leaves ;

—Polybius, 242 leaves ;—2 leaves for register and anchor.

The Florus and Polybius are often found alone.

177. APOLLONIJ rhodij Argonautica, antiquis unà, & optimis cum commentarijs. *Graece.* Aprili. M. D. XXI.   8vo.

Collation : 228 leaves.

Very rare.

178.   *(Didymi)* · INTERPRETA-TIONES et antiquæ et perquam utiles in Homeri Iliada, nec non in Odyssea. *Graece.*   8vo.

Collation : 320 leaves.

179. PORPHYRIJ philosophi homeri-carum quæstionum liber. Eiusdem de Nympharum antro in Odyssea, opusculum. *Graece.*   Maio. M. D. XXI.   8vo.

Collation: 44 leaves.

180.   C. SUETONIJ Tranquilli xii Cæsares, etc.   Majo. M. D. XXI.   8vo.

Collation : lx and 320 leaves.

A copy on vellum was in the La Valière sale, No. 4937.

181. L. APVLEII Metamorphoseos, siue lusus Asini libri xi, etc.   Majo M. D. XXI. 8vo.

Collation : 294 leaves.

182. TERENTIVS. Ivnio. M. D. XXI. 8vo.

Collation : xvi and 147 leaves.

183. IL PETRARCA.—*Impresso in Vinegia nelle case d'Aldo Romano, e d'Andrea Asolano suo suocero nell' anno M. D. XXI. del mese di Giulio.* 8vo.

A reprint of the 1501 edition.

184. RHETORICORUM ad Herennium lib. iiii., etc. Octobri M. D. XXI. 4to.

Collation : xvi and 246 leaves.

185. HORÆ Beatæ Virginis. Psalmi pœnitentiales. *Graece.* 1521. 32mo.

A very rare reprint of the edition of 1505.

In 1522, Andrea d'Asola published 10 works :

186. TROGI Pompei externae Historiae in compendivm ab Ivstino redactae. Externorum imperatorum uitæ authore Aemylio Probo. Ian. M. D. XXII. 8vo.

Collation: 204 leaves.

Very rare.

187. L. ANNEI Senecae natvralivm qvaestionvm libri vii. Febrvario. M. D. XXII. 4to.

Collation : vi and 136 leaves.

One of the the very rarest of the productions of the Aldine Press.

188. M. T. C. Epistolae familiares accvrativs recognitae. Ivnio. M. D. XXII. 8vo.

Collation : 272 leaves.

Nearly as rare as the 1512 edition.

189. EX Plavti Comoediis. xx. qvarvm carmina magna ex parte in mensvm svvm restitvta svnt. Ivlio. M. D. XXII. 4to.

Collation : xiv and 284 leaves.

Not a rare edition.

190. GVILLIELMI Bvdaei Parisiensis Secretarij Regij libri v de Asse, & partib. eius post duas Parisienses impressiones ab eodem ipso Budæo castigati, idq; authore Io. Grolierio Lugdunensi Christianissimi Gallorum Regis Secretario, et Galicarum copiarum Quæstore, cui etiam ob nostram in eum observantiam à nobis illi dicantur. Septembri. M. D. xxii. 4to.

Collation : xii and 264 leaves.

A copy on vellum, with coloured initials, appears in the Soubise Catalogue, No. 8010.

191. LVCIANI dialogi et alia mvlta opera, etc. Octobri. M. D. XXII. Folio.

Collation : x and 572 pages, the last, owing to an error commencing page 450, being numbered 271.

Care should be taken to see if pages 385-392

and 435-440 have not been torn out, as they were suppressed by the Inquisition.

192. IL Decamerone di. M. Giovanni Boccaccio novamente corretto con tre novelle aggivnte.—*Impresso in Vinegia nelle Case d'Aldo Romano, & d'Andrea Asolano suo suocero nell' anno M. D. XXII. Del mese di Nouembre.* 4to.

Collation: 326 leaves.

193. PETRI. Alcyonii. Medices. Lega-tvs. De. Exsilio. Novembri. M. D. xxii. 4to.

Collation: 70 leaves.

Very rare. The author is accused of having embodied in it Cicero's De Gloria, and of having then destroyed the only existing MS. of this now lost work.

194. NICANDRI Theriaca.   Eiusdem Alexipharmaca.   Interpretatio innominati authoris in Theriaca.   Commentarii diuer-sorum authorum in Alexipharmaca.   Ex-positio ponderum, mensurarum, signorum, & characterum. *Graece.* 4to.

Collation: 92 leaves.

The commentaries bear the date of 1523.

195. ASCONII Paediani expositio in iiii.   Orationes M. Tvllii Cic., etc.   De-cembri. M. D. XXII.   8vo.

Collation: xii and 284 leaves.

The following year gave birth to seven works :

196. CL. CLAVDIANI opera quam diligentissime castigata, qvorvm indicem in seqventi pagina . reperies. Martio M. D. XXIII. 8vo.

Collation: 176 leaves.

197. GEORGII Trapezuntii Rhetoricorum libri v., etc. Aprili. M. D. XXIII. Folio.

Collation: iv and 162 leaves.

198. C. VALERII Flacci Argonavtica. Io. Baptistæ Pij carmen ex quarto Argonauticon Apollonij. Orphei Argonautica innominato interprete. Maio. M. D. XXIII. 8vo.

Collation: 148 leaves.

199. M. T. CICERONIS de philosophia volvmen primvm, in qvo haec continentvr, etc. Maio. M. D. XXIII. 8vo

Collation: viii and 256 leaves.

200. SECVNDO volvmine haec continentvr. M. T. C. de natura Deorum libri iii., etc. Avgvsto. M. D. XXIII. 8vo.

Collation: 216 leaves.

Extremely rare.

201. SILII Italici de Bello Pvnico

secvndo xvii libri nvper diligentissime castigati. Ivlio. M. D. XXIII. 8vo.

Collation: 212 leaves.

202. ALDI Pii Manvtii Institvtionvm Grammaticarvm libri qvatvor. Erasmi Roterodami opusculum de octo orationis partium constructione. Ivlio. M. D. XXIII. 4to.

Collation: viii and 204 leaves, followed by the same appendix as in the 1501, 1508, and 1514 editions.

Under the date of 1524, I can only trace three works, viz :

203. HOMERI opera omnia. *Graece.* Aprili. M. D. XXIIII. 2 vol. 8vo.

Collation : Vol. i., 278 leaves ; vol. ii., 252 leaves.

Very inferior to the editions of 1504 and 1517, and not nearly so rare.

204. HERODIANI historiarum lib. viii. græce pariter, & latine. M. D. XXIIII. 8vo.

Collation: iv and 190 leaves.

205. DICTIONARIVM graecvm cum interpretatione latina, omnium, quæ hactenus impressa sunt, copiosissimum, etc. Decembri. M. D. XXIIII. Folio.

Collation: Part i., 148 leaves ; Part ii., 165 leaves.

Not so rare as the edition of 1497.

In 1525, the Aldine Press produced again three works, viz.:

206. XENOPHONTIS omnia, qvae extant. *Graece.* Aprili. M. D. xxv. Folio.

Collation: iv and 87 leaves, after which come 2 blank leaves, followed by 116 leaves of text and 1 leaf with anchor. Leaves 84 and 85 are wrongly numbered 85 and 86.

207. THEODORI (*Gazae*) Grammatices libri. iiii. De mensibus liber eiusdem. Georgii Lecapeni de constructione uerborum. Emmanuelis moschopuli de constructione nominum, & uerborum. Eiusdem de accentibus. *Graece.* Iunio. M. D. xxv. 8vo.

Collation: 238 leaves.

Very rare.

208. GALENI opera omnia. *Graece,* M. D. xxv. 5 vols. Folio.

Collation: Vol. i., 316 leaves in all; vol. ii., 294 leaves in all (the last numbered 160 instead of 106); vol. iii., 266 leaves in all; vol. iv., 247 leaves in all; vol. v., 337 leaves in all.

Renouard gives a most elaborate collation of each volume, but I believe the above will answer every purpose.

In 1526, again, only three works appeared:

209. SIMPLICII Commentarii. Ianuario M. D. xxvi. Folio.

Collation: iv and 178 leaves.

210. OMNIA Opera Hippocratis. *Graece.* Maii. M. D. XXVI. Folio.

Collation: vi and 234 leaves.

Editio princeps. Rare.

211. SIMPLICII Commentarii in octo Aristotelis physicae Avscvltationis libros cvm ipso Aristotelis textv. *Graece.* Octobri. M. D. XXVI. Folio.

Collation: iv and 322 leaves.

Eight works were issued in 1527, viz.:

212. NICOLAI Perotti Cornucopiae latinae. Folio.

Collation: clxiv. and 750 pages. The date of 1526 appears at foot of columns 1054 and 1436, and that of 1527 on the last page.

213. PRISCIANI grammatici Caesariensis libri omnes. Maio. M. D. XXVII. 4to.

Collation: xiv and 302 leaves.

214. VIRGILIVS. Ivnio. M. D. XXVII. 8vo.

Collation: 220 leaves.

215. VLPIANI commentarioli in olynthiacas, philippicas'q; Demosthenis orationes, etc. *Graece.* Ivnio M. D. XXVII. Folio.

Collation: 120 leaves.

216. SIMPLICII Commentaria in tres

libros Aristotelis de anima, etc.   *Graece.*
Ivnio M. D. XXVII.   Folio.

Collation : iv and 188 leaves.

217. ACTII Synceri Sannazarii de
Partv Virginis, etc.   Avgvsto. M. D. XXVII.
8vo.

Collation : viii and 48 leaves.

218. IOANNES Grammaticvs (*Philo-
ponus*) in libros de Generatione, etc.
Graece. Septembri. M. D. XXVII.   Folio.

Collation : ii and 148 leaves.

219. Q. H. FL. POEMATA omnia.
Septembri M. D. XXVII.   8vo.

Collation : As in the edition of 1519.

Andrea d'Asola published six works in 1528 :

220. AVRELII Cornelii Celsi Medi-
cinae libri. viii. Martio. M. D. XXVIII.   4to.

Collation : viii and 164 leaves.

221. MACROBII in Somnivm Scipionis, etc.   Aprili M. D. XXVIII.   8vo.

Collation : xvi and 324 leaves.

222. IL libro del Cortegiano del Conte
Baldesar Castiglione.—*In Venetia nelle
case d'Aldo Romano, & d'Andrea d'Asola
suo Suocero, nell' anno M. D. XXVIII.
del mese d'Aprile.*   Folio.

Collation : 122 leaves.

Editio princeps. · Rare.

223. DIDYMI antiqvissimi avctoris interpretatio in Odysseam. *Graece.* Ivnio. M. D. XXVIII.   8vo.

Collation : 128 leaves.

224. PAVLI Aeginetae medici optimi, libri septem. *Graece.* Avgvsto. M. D. XXVIII. Folio.

Collation : iv and 140 leaves.

Editio princeps.

225. ACTII Synceri Sannazarii de Partv Virginis, etc.   Avgvsto, M. D. XXVIII. 8vo.

Collation : 67 leaves.

Only one work bears the date of 1529 :

226. RECOGNITIO Veteris Testamenti ad hebraicam veritatem, etc. M D XXIX.   4to.

Collation : ii and 212 leaves.

Andrea d'Asola died in 1529. After his death long disputes between his sons and those of Aldus the Elder caused the Press to stand idle for four years, and it was only in 1533 that work was resumed, under the direction of Paulus Manutius, and in the joint interest of himself, his brothers, and the heirs of Andrea.

PAULUS MANUTIUS.

URING the years that Andrea d'Asola had managed the undertaking, the children of Aldus were growing up. For the first few years they remained under the guardianship of their mother at Asola, but they were soon removed to Venice, where Paul especially was received with open arms by his father's old friends, Bembo, Ramberto, Egnatio, and others. He devoted himself to study with such ardour that he seriously injured his health, and for two years had to give up work of every description. Having recovered his strength, he experienced great annoyance from the disputes which arose between his uncles and himself as to the working of the printing establishment, *domesticas controversias*, as he calls them in a letter to his friend Saulius (Ep. i. 3). From 1529 to 1533 the Press remained inactive, but in the latter year Paulus Manutius, though only 21 years of age, took the management into his own hands, and we now find that most, if not all, the works issuing from his Press bear the imprint "In Aedibus Haeredum Aldi et Andreæ Asulani Soceri." I shall not quote the imprint in future, and, as I now trust the reader has understood the plan I am following, I shall also omit the repetition of the word "*Collation*," though I shall continue to give the Collation itself after the size of each volume. The date will be given at the head of the list of publications for each year, but will not be repeated after each work.

M. D. XXXIII.

227. RHETORICORUM ad C. Herennium lib. iiii etc. 4to. xvi and 246 leaves.

228. IL LIBRO del Cortegiano del Conte Baldesar Castiglione. 8vo. 216 leaves.

229. TITI Livii Patavini Decadis qvintae libri qvinqve. 8vo. 136 leaves.

230. IL PETRARCA. · 8vo: 184 leaves ;—44 leaves for supplement ;—1 blank leaf ;—table of contents ;—1 blank leaf ; — Preface *a' Lettori ;* — Life of *Madonna Laura ;*—Notes on Petrarch.

231. JOANNIS Joviani Pontani carmina. Tomus primus. 8vo. 256 leaves.

The date appears on leaf 247.

232. M. T. C. EPISTOLAE familiares. 8vo. 287 leaves.

233. P. OVIDII Nasonis Opera omnia. 8vo. Vol. i., xxxii and 204 leaves; vol. ii., xii and 180 leaves ; vol. iii., xxiv and 232 leaves.

234. LIBRI de Re rvstica. 4to. liv. and 296 leaves.

235. L'ANTHROPOLOGIA di Galeazzo Capella. 8vo. 75 leaves.

236. ACTII Synceri Sannazarii de partv Virginis Libri iii. 8vo. iv and 100 leaves.

M. D. XXXIV.

237. POETÆ tres egregij nunc primum in lucem editi. 8vo. vi. and 46 leaves.

The three poets are Gratius, Nemesianus and a fragment of Ovid. Rare.

238. DIVERSORVM vetervm poetarvm in Priapvm Lvsvs. 8vo. 80 leaves.

239. VALERIVS Maximvs. 8vo. xvi. and 211 leaves.

240. OMNIA Themistii Opera. Folio. 174 leaves.

Editio princeps.

241. ISOCRATES. Folio. 116 leaves.

242. ARCADIA del Sannazaro. 8vo. 92 leaves.

243. SONETTI, è Canzoni del ·Sannazaro. 8vo. 52 leaves.

244. AETII Amideni Librorvm Medicinalivm tomvs primvs. *Graece.* Folio. iv. and 178 leaves.

245. CORNELIUS Tacitvs. 4to. xii and 260 leaves.

246. IOANNIS Grammatici in posteriora resolvtoria Aristotelis, Commentarivm. Folio. · 192 leaves.

M. D. XXXV.

247. IVVENALIS. PERSIVS. 8vo. 78 leaves.

248. L. COELII Lactantii Firmiani divinarvm institvtionvm libri septem. 8vo.

248*a*. IACOBI Sannazarii opera omnia. 8vo. 104 leaves.

Superior to the earlier editions.

249. C. PLINII Secvndi natvralis Historiae secvnda pars. 8vo. 304 leaves.

The second volume was thus published before the first, which is dated 1536.

M. D. XXXVI.

250. C. PLINII Secvndi natvralis Historiae prima pars. 8vo. xlviii. and 314 leaves.

251. TERTIA pars. 8vo. 296 leaves.

The three volumes together are extremely rare and valuable.

252. LAVRENTII Vallae Elegantiarvm libri sex. 4to. viii and 200 leaves.

253. ARISTOTELIS Poetica. 8vo. 56 leaves.

Very rare.

254. GREGORII Nazanzeni Theologi Orationes. 8vo. 228 leaves.

255. EVSTRATII Commentaria. Folio. ii. and 190 leaves.

In this year (1536) Manutius was called to Rome. He there became acquainted with Marcello Cervino, afterwards Pope Marcellus II. He seems to have been away during the whole of the year 1537, and to have only returned in 1538, in which year he only issued one book.

―――――

M. D. XXXVIII.

256. INDEX in C. Plinii Nat. Hist. libros. 8vo. 251 leaves.

C

This very rare volume completes the Pliny. It is printed in two columns with a poor type.

At the end of 1538 Manutius again left Venice, and spent some time in visiting the ancient libraries of Italy. In 1540 the connection between him and his uncles ceased, and henceforth nearly all his books bear the imprint *Apud Aldi filios.*

———·——

M. D. XL.

257. C. PLINII naturalis Historiae pars prima et secunda. 2 vols 8vo.

This is nothing more nor less than the volumes issued in 1535 and 1536, with a new date. This is proved by the fact that even the broken letters are the same in both editions.

258. HISTORIE di Nicolò Machiavelli. 8vo. iv and 260 leaves.

259. LIBRO dell' arte della gverra di Nicolò Machiavelli, etc. 8vo. ii and 118 leaves.

260. IL Prencipe di Nicolò Machiavelli. 8vo. ii and 85 leaves.

261. DISCORSI di Nicolò Machiavelli. 8vo. viii and 216 leaves.

It is very rare to find the 4 vols. of Machiavelli together.

262. M. TVLLII Ciceronis Epistolae familiares. 8vo. iv. and 318 leaves.

263. M. TVLLII Ciceronis Epistolae ad Atticum, etc. 8vo. ii and 367 leaves.
Some vellum copies are known.

264. M. TULLII Ciceronis Orationes. 3 vols. 8vo. Vol. i., iv. and 305. Vol. ii., 282. Vol. iii., 271.

M. D. XLI.

265. MARCI Tvllii Ciceronis Officiorvm libri tres. 8vo. ii and 134.

266. M. TVLLII Ciceronis de Philosophia, prima pars. 8vo. iv. and 252.

267. M. TVLLII Cicaronis de Philosophia volvmen secvndvm. 8vo. iii and 214 leaves.

268. VIRGILIVS. 8vo. 224 leaves.

269. TERENTII Comoediae. 8vo. xvi and 146 leaves.

270. BARTHOLOMAEI Riccii de Imitatione. 8vo. 88 leaves.

271. REGOLE grammaticali della volgar lingva, di Messer Francesco Fortvnio. 8vo. iv and 48 leaves.

This is the first book published on the formation of the Italian tongue.

272. IL libro del Cortegiano del conte Baldesar Castiglione. 8vo. 200 leaves.

273. DIALOGI di Amore,. composti per Leone medico. 8vo. 264 leaves.

274. COMMENTARII delle cose de Tvrchi, di Pavlo Giovio, et Andrea Gambini, con gli fatti, et la vita di Scanderberg. 8vo. 128 leaves.

275. STANZE di Messer Angelo Poli tiano. 8vo. 32 leaves.

Extremely rare.

M. D. XLII.

276. HIERONYMI Ferrarii ad Pavlvm Manvtivm emendationes in Philippicas Ciceronis. 8vo. 126 leaves.

277. COMMENTARII in Epistolas Pavli, ad Romanos, et ad Galatas. 4to. 174 leaves.

These commentaries were written by Marino Grimani.

278. LETTERE volgari di diversi nobilissimi hvomini. 8vo. 192 leaves.

This is the first vol. of this collection of letters.

279. AMBROSII Calepini Dictiona- vm. Folio.

280. EXQVISITAE in Porphirivm

Commentationes Danielis Barbari.   4to.
110 leaves.

281. DIALOGHI di M. Sperone
Speroni. 8vo.

This book was reprinted in 1543-4-6-50-2.

M. D. XLIII.

282. M. TVLLII Ciceronis Epistolae
ad familiares, &c. 8vo.

An exact reprint of the 1540 edition.

283. LE RICHEZZE della lingva
volgare di M. Francesco Alvnno. Folio.
226 leaves.

284. DIALOGHI di M. S. Speroni.
8vo. 172 leaves.

285. LETTERE volgari di diuersi
nobilissimi hvomini. 8vo.

A reprint of the edition of the previous year.

286. ORBECCHE tragedia di M.
Giovanbattista Giraldi Cinthio da Ferrara.
8vo. 64 leaves.

287. SOLI DEO honor et gloria.
Recens lvtheranarvm assertionvm oppvg-
natio, per Magistrvm Petrvm Avrelivm
Sanvtvm Venetvm Avgvstinianvm. 4to.
104 leaves.

288. VIAGGI fatti da Vinetia, alla
Tana, in Persia, etc. 8vo. 180 leaves.

M. D. XLIV.

289. M. TVLLII Ciceronis Epistolae ad Atticum, etc. 8vo. 350 leaves.

290. DELLA vera tranqvillità dell' animo. Opera utilissima, and nuouamente composta dalla Illustrissima Signora la Signora Isabella Sforza. 4to. 54 leaves.

291. LETTERE Volgari, &c. libro primo. 8vo. 184 leaves.

292. DIALOGHI di M. Speron Speroni. 8vo. 160 leaves.

M. D. XLV.

293. CICERO de Officiis, de Senectute, de Amicitia, &c. 8vo. 130 leaves.

294. REGOLE grammaticali della volgar lingva, di messer Francesco Fortvnio. 8vo. 46 leaves.

295. DE Discorsi del Reverendo Monsignor Francesco Patritij. 8vo. 282 leaves.

296. LA Hypnerotomachia di Poliphilo. Folio. 234 leaves.

297. APPIANO Alessandrino delle gverre civili et esterne de Romani. 8vo. Part i., 258 leaves. Part ii., 176 leaves. Part iii., 42 leaves.

298. BARTHOLOMAEI Riccii de Imitatione. 8vo. 88 leaves.

299. LETTERE volgari. 8vo.

There are two editions of the 2nd vol. of the Lettere Volgari under this date. The 1st has 130 leaves, the 2nd 136.

300. VIRGILIVS. 8vo. 220 leaves.

301. M. ANTONII Flaminii in librvm Psalmorvm brevis explanatio. 8vo. 278 leaves.

302. VIAGGI alla Tana, in Persia, etc. 8vo. 164 leaves.

303. IL Libro del Cortegiano del conte Baldessar Castiglione. Folio. 122 leaves.

304. ORLANDO Fvrioso di Messer Lodovico Ariosto, et di piv aggivntovi in fine piv di cinqvecento Stanze del medesimo Avtorre, non piv vedvte.—*In Venetia, In casa de' figlivoli d' Aldo.* 4to. 276 leaves.

One of the rarest of all the Aldine publications.

305. DIALOGHI di Amore. 8vo. 264 leaves.

306. LE Epistole famigliari di Cicerone. 8vo. 334 leaves.

There seems to be a 2nd edition under the same date with only 305 leaves.

307. P. TERENTII Afri Comoediae. 8vo. 164 leaves.

308. BERNARDINI Parthenii Foroivliensis pro lingva latina Oratio. 4to. 46 leaves.

M. D. XLVI.

309. M. TVLLII Ciceronis Orationes. 3 vols. 8vo. Vol. i., 308 leaves. Yol. ii., 282 leaves. Vol. iii., 272 leaves.

310. M. TVLLII Ciceronis de Philosophia, prima pars. 8vo. 272 leaves.

311. M. TVLLII Ciceronis de Philosophia volvmen secvndvm. 8vo. 231 leaves.

312. RHETORICORVM ad C. Herennivm libri iiii. 8vo. 422 leaves.

313. M. T. CICERONIS Defensiones contra Celii Calcagnini disquisitiones in eius officia. 8vo. 76 leaves.

314. IN omnes de arte Rhetorica M. Tvllii Ciceronis libros, doctissimorvm virorvm Commentaria. Folio. Part i., xx and 312 pp. Part ii., 414 pp.

315. M. TVLLII Ciceronis Epistolae familiares. 8vo. 272 leaves and 40 for the notes.

316. IL Principe di Nicolò Machiavelli. 8vo.

317. DISCORSI di Nicolò Machiavelli. 8vo. 216 leaves.

318. LIBRO dell' arte della gverra di Nicolo Machiavelli. 8vo. 112 leaves.

319. HISTORIE di Nicolò Machiavelli. 8vo. 248 leaves.

320. SCIPIONIS Capicii de Principiis rervm. 8vo. 64 leaves.

321. LETTERE volgari, &c. 8vo. 136 leaves.

A reprint of the first volume.

322. COMMENTARIA in primam D. Ioannis Epistolam, Io. Baptista Folengio Monacho Mantvano avctore. 8vo. xii and 162 leaves.

323. VITA, Gesti, Costvmi, Discorsi, lettere di Marco Aurelio imperatore. 8vo. 152 leaves.

324. PRETIOSA Margarita. 8vo. xx and 218 leaves.

Rare, especially in good condition.

325. LE Occorrenze hvmane per Nicolo Libvrnio composte. 8vo. xii and 145 leaves.

326. FRANCISCI Philippi Pedimontii

Ecphrasis in Horatii Flacci Artem poeti-
cam.   4to.   66 leaves.

327. FERDINANDI Abdvensis contra
iurisprudentiæ uituperatores Oratio.   8vo.
47 leaves.

328. AMMONII Hermiae in Qvinque
voces Porphyrii Commentarivs.   8vo.   iv
and 80 leaves.

329. AMMONII Hermiae in Predica-
ménta Aristotelis Commentarivs.   8vo.
152 leaves.

330. AMMONII Hermiae in Aristotelis
de Interpretatione Librvm Commentarivs.
8vo.   188 leaves.

331. ANDREAE Alciati Emblematvm
Libellvs.   8vo.   48 leaves ; 84 woodcuts.
Very rare.

332. IL Petrarca.   8vo.   194 leaves.

333. DIALOGHI di M. Speron
Speroni.   8vo.   160 leaves.

334. LE Comedie di Terentio.   8vo.
168 leaves.

In 1546 Paulus Manutius married Margherita
Odoni, by whom he had three sons and one
daughter.   The eldest he named Aldus, after his
father, and he often mentions his daughter in his

letters, but of his other sons we only know that the
second, named Girolamo, died at the age of nine.

M. D. XLVII.

335. IN Epistolas Ciceronis ad Atticvm,
Pavli Manvtii Commentarivs.   8vo.   vi
and 470 leaves.

336. ASCONII Pediani expositio in
iiii. orationes M. Tullij Ciceronis.   8vo.
106 leaves.

337. IN omnes M. Tvllii Ciceronis
Orationes doctissimorvm virorvm Lvcvbrationes.   Folio.   367 leaves.

338. COMMENTARII di Caio Givlio
Cesare.   8vo.   257 leaves.

339. DIDONE, Tragedia di M. Lodovico Dolce.   8vo.   42 leaves.

340. BERNARDI Georgii Epitome
Principvm Venetorvm.   4to.

In the Pinelli sale, No. 5328, was a copy on
vellum.

341. IL libro del Cortegiano.   8vo.
208 leaves.

Editio Aldina optima.

342. MEDICI antiqvi omnes.   Folio.
332 leaves in all.

M. D. XLVIII.

343. EPISTOLE famigliari di Cicerone. 8vo. 306 leaves.

344. M. TVLLII Ciceronis Epistolae ad Atticum. 8vo. ii and 346 leaves.

345. CICERO de Officiis, de Senectute, de Amicitia, etc. 8vo. ii and 134 leaves.

346. LETTERE volgari. 8vo. 120 leaves.

This is only the second volume of the collection.

347. AMBROSII Calepini Dictiona-rivm, cum additamentis Pavli Manvtii. Folio.

A reprint of the 1542 edition.

348. PETRI Paschalii adversvs Ioannis Mavlii Parricidas Actio, in Senatu Veneto recitata. 8vo. 166 leaves.

Rare.

M. D. XLIX.

349. DEMOSTHENIS Orationes qva-tvor contra Philippum à Paulo Manutio latinitate donatæ. 4to. 52 leaves.

Rare.

350. GIOCASTA. Tragedia di M. Lodovico Dolce. 8vo. 56 leaves.

351. FABRITIA. Comedia di M. Lodovico Dolce. 60 leaves.

352. EPISTOLE famigliari di Cicerone, &c. 8vo.

A reprint of the *second* edition of 1545.

353. LETTERE volgari. 8vo. 136 leaves.

354. DIALOGHI di amore. 8vo. 228 leaves.

355. FRANCISCI Priscianensis argvmentorvm observationes in omneis Ciceronis epistolas. 8vo. 64 leaves.

A scarce book.

356. MAGNVM Etymologicvm Græcæ linguæ. *Venetiis* apvd *Federicvm Tvrrisanvm*. Folio. 176 leaves.

Though bearing only the name of Frederick Torresano, it is undoubtedly printed by Paulus Manutius. After having tried several printers, Frederick renewed his commercial transactions with Manutius in 1549. In 1558 his sons or nephews started a press of their own, adopting for their imprint the formula *in* or *ex Bibliotheca Aldina*, which one of them, Bernardo Torresano, had used in Paris, whence he had just returned after having been a bookseller there about twelve years.

The book is rare.

357. EROTEMATA Chrysolorae. 8vo. 381 leaves.

The eighth leaf of sig. S is blank and is not counted.

358. PLATONIS, Thvcydidis, et Demosthenis fvnebres Orationes. *Graece*. 8vo. 48 leaves.

Very rare.

———

M. D. L.

359. M. TULLII Ciceronis Opera Rhetorica. 8vo.

An exact reprint of the 1546 edition.

360. M. T. CICERONIS Orationes. 8vo.

An exact reprint of the 1546 edition.

361. FLORILEGIVM. 8vo. 300 leaves.

362. GREGORII Orationes ii. 8vo.

363. COMEDIA del Sacrificio degli Intronati. 8vo.

364. DIALOGHI di M. Speron Speroni. 8vo. 144 leaves.

365. LETTERE volgari. 8vo. 120 leaves.

366. DOMITII Marini Carmina. 4to.

367. DELLE lettere di M. Pietro

Bembo secondo volvme. 8vo. x. and 172 leaves.

The first vol. of these letters appeared at Rome in 1548, 4to., and the 3rd and 4th at Venice, *apud Gualtero Scotto*, 1552, 8vo.

368. IOANNIS Baptistæ Camotii Philosophi Commentaria. Folio. 114 leaves.

Very rare.

369. IVNIORIS Lvdovici Pariseti Regiensis, ad Varivm Tolomaevm Theopoeiae libri sex. 8vo. 124 leaves,

370. METHODVS in Aphorismos Hippocratis. 4to.

371. AMBROSII Calepini Diction- arivm. Folio.

M. D. LI.

372. M. T. CICERONIS Epistolae ad Atticum &c. 8vo.

A reprint of the 1548 edition.

373. LE Epistole famigliari di Cicerone, &c. 8vo. 306 leaves.

374. IN omnes de arte Rhetorica Ciceronis libros Commentaria, &c. Eolio.

A reprint of the edition of 1546.

375 NATALIS Comitvm Veneti de Venatione, libri iiii. 8vo. 48 leaves.

Rare.

376. PETRI Bembi Cardinalis Historiæ Venetae libri xii. Folio. iv. and 204 leaves.

377. VICTORIS Favsti Veneti Orationes. 4to. 90 leaves.

Editio princeps. Rare.

378. ARISTOTELIS Opera omnia, 1551-52-53. 6 vols., 8vo. Vol. i., xx. and 679 pages; vol. ii., xvi and 438 pages; vol. iii., xxxii and 948 pages; vol. iv., xvi and 607 pages; vol. v., xxiv and 648 pages; vol. vi., xvi and 654 pages;—1 blank leaf.

A very valuable edition, rarely found complete.

379. APPIANO Alessandrino. 3 parts in 1 vol. 8vo.

A reprint of the edition of 1545.

380. OLYMPIODORI in Meteora Aristotelis Commentarii. 2 vols., Folio. Vol. i., 108; vol. ii., 144.

381. LE Richezze della lingva volgare. Folio. 220 leaves.

382. DEMOSTHENIS Orationes. 4to. 52 leaves.

383. LETTERE volgari di diversi, etc. 2 vols, 8vo. Vol. i., 136; vol ii., 120 leaves.

384. OPERE di M. Pietro Aretino. 4to. 200 leaves.

385. DIONIS Chrysostomi Orationes lxxx. 8vo. 456 leaves.

Printed *after* 1550 and *before* 1552.   It bears no date or imprint.

M. D. LII.

386. CICERONIS opera philosophica. 2 vols., 8vo.

A reprint of the 1546 edition.

387. CICERONIS de Officiis. 8vo.

A reprint of the 1541 edition.

388. IN omnes M. Tvllii Ciceronis Orationes doctissimorvm virorvm Lvcvbrationes. Folio. 731 pages.

389. AMBROSII Calepini Dictionarium. Folio.

390. REGOLE grammaticali di Messer Francesco Fortvnio. 8vo. 46 leaves.

391. LE Epistole famigliari di Cicerone. 8vo. 306 leaves.

392. DIALOGHI di amore. 8vo. 228 leaves.

393. DIALOGHI di M. Speron Speroni. 8vo. 144 leaves.

394. LE Istorie fiorentine di Nic. Machiavelli, &c. 8vo.

395. IVNIORIS Lvdovici Orationes tres. 8vo. 240 leaves.

396. PIETRO Aretino. Vite. 4to.

397. ADEODATI Oratio. 4to.

M. D. LIII.

398. ASCONII Pediani Expositio. 8vo. 104 leaves.

399. IN Epistolam Q. Horatii Flacci de Arte poetica interpretatio. 8vo. 166 leaves.

Mitscherlich, in his list of editions of Horace, says he had a copy of this edition with the imprint of J. Arrivabene, of Venice, 1553.

400. IL sacro Regno de'l gran Patritio. 8vo. xxiv and 368 leaves.

401. IN Epistolas Ciceronis ad Atticvm, Pavli Manvtii Commentarivs. 8vo. 418 leaves.

402. P. TERENTII Afri Comoediae. 8vo. xvi and 152 leaves.

403. LVDOVICI Pariseti Ivnioris Epistolarvm posteriorvm libri tres. 8vo.

404. STANZE pastorali di Baldassare Castiglione, e Cesare Gonzaga ; con le Rime di Ant. Giacomo Corso.

Rare.

405. S. GREGORII Nazianzeni Commentarivs. 8vo. ✻

406. PAULI Æginetæ opera. 8vo.

407. MATTHAEI Gribaldi Mophae Interpretationes in l. ii. C. Commu. de Lega. et in L. Verbis Legis de Verbor. significat. 8vo.

In this year Manutius made another voyage to Rome and stayed there a couple of months.

M. D. LIV.

408. NICOLAI Liburnii Veneti Epithalamivm. 4to.

409. ORIBASII Sardiani Synopseos ad Evstathivm filivm libri novem. 8vo. 216 leaves.

410. PSELLI Philosophi in Physicen Aristotelis Commentarii. Folio. vi and 82 leaves.

411. FRANCISCI Lvisini in librvm Q. Horatii Flacci de Arte poetica Commentarivs. 4to. 88 leaves.

412. I QVATTRO primi libri di Archi-

tettvra di Pietro Cataneo Senese. Large-folio. 58 leaves.

413. DI S. Giovanni Crisostomo Libri tre della Prouidenza di Dio. 8vo. 162 leaves.

414. IOVITAE ' Rapicii de Nvmero. Folio. 76 leaves.

415. SANCTI Ioannis Damasceni adversvs sanctarvm imaginvm oppvgnatores. 8vo. 100 leaves.

416. DEMOSTHENIS Orationvm pars prima. 8vo. Part i., viii and 124 leaves; part ii., 252 leaves; part iii., ii. and 245 leaves.

417. DVE Orationi, I'vna di Eschine, I'altra di Demosthene. 8vo. 108 leaves.

418. POESIE volgari, di Lorenzo de' Medici. 8vo. 208 leaves.

Leaves 105 to 112 are often missing, as they contain two somewhat free poems.

419. TRACTATVS de Nvllitatibvs, etc. 8vo. viii and 326 leaves.

420. BARTHOLOMAEI Fvmi Svmma. 8vo. viii and 468 leaves.

421. LETTERE volgari. 8vo. 145 leaves.

422. M. T. CICERONIS Epistolae ad familiares. 8vo.

423. LE Epistole famigliari di Cicerone. 8vo. 320 leaves.

424. M. TVLLII Ciceronis Epistolae ad Atticvm. 8vo. ii and 346 leaves.

425 M. TVLLII Ciceronis Orationes. 3 vols. 8vo. Vol. i., 328 leaves : vol. ii., iii. and 296 leaves : vol. iii., iii. and 292 leaves.

426. RHETORICORVM ad C. Herennivm libri iiii. 8vo. 184 leaves.

427. CICERONIS de Oratore, etc. 8vo. 248 leaves, wrongly numbered.

428. CATVLLVS. 8vo. iv and 138 leaves, wrongly numbered.

429. EGNATII de exemplis illustrium virorum Venetae Civitatis, atque aliarum gentium liber. 8vo.

430. OMNIVM Caesarvm verissimae Imagines ex antiqvis nvmismatis desvmptae. 4to. 77 leaves.
Very rare.

431. ORATIONE di Cicerone, in difesa di Milone. 8vo. 40 leaves.

432. BERNARDINI Lavredani Oratio. 4to.

During 1554 the health of Manutius again gave way, and his eyesight became affected. This, no doubt, is the reason why his subsequent productions are inferior to those issued up to this date.

M. D. LV.

433. ORATIONE di Demosthene contra la legge di Lettine. 8vo. 32 leaves wrongly numbered.

434. TERENTIVS. 8vo. 205 leaves.

435. REGVM, Consvlvm, Dictatorvm, ac Censorvm Romanorvm Fasti. Folio. 34 leaves.

Editio princeps. Extremely rare.

436. M. T. CICERONIS Opera philosophica. 2 vols., 8vo. Vol. i., iv and 276 leaves; vol. ii., 264 leaves in all, folio i. having been forgotten.

437. CICERONIS de Officiis. 8vo. 148 leaves.

438. LE Pistole di Cicerone ad Attico. 8vo. 400 leaves.

Renouard mentions an edition without a date : it is probable that he possessed a copy with a title-page printed some years later.

439. CAROLI SIGONII Pro Eloquentia Orationes iiii. 4to. iv and 32 leaves.

440. HIERONYMI Ragazonii in epistolas Ciceronis familiares Commentarivs.
8vo. xii and 88 leaves.

441. OPVS Thomae Campegii. 8vo.

442. M. ANTONII Mvreti Orationes.
4to. 20 leaves.

443. MOSCHI, Bionis, Theocriti Carmina. 4to. 28 leaves.

444. DIONYSII Longini de svblimi
genere dicendi. 4to. 24 leaves.

Very rare.

445. T. LIVII Patavini, libri. Folio.
iv and 616 leaves.

Editio Aldina optima. Extremely Rare.

446. HORATIVS. 8vo. viii and 180
leaves.

Editions have been quoted by Mitscherlich
bearing the dates of 1551, 52, and 57 but he has
evidently copied from *Bibl. Horatiana*, 1775, 8vo.

The error is proved by the fact that he quotes
the imprint of all as being *Apud Aldum Jun.*,
and Aldus the younger was only born in 1547,
being thus only 4 years old in 1551, 6 in 1553,
and 10 in 1557.

447. VIRGILIVS. 8vo.

In this year Manutius went to Bologna to see
his brother Antonio. There he was taken ill and

had to remain a considerable time. The Bolognese offered him advantageous terms to remove his press to their city, which, after some hesitation, he finally declined.

M. D. LVI.

448. EPISTOLAE clarorvm virorvm. 8vo. 132 leaves.

449. LETTERE volgari. 8vo. 120 leaves.

450. M. T. CICERONIS Epistolae ad familiares. 8vo.

A reprint of the last edition.

451. L'EPISTOLE di M. Tullio Cicerone, scritte a M. Bruto. 8vo.

452. LE Filippiche di Marco T. Cicerone Contra Marco Antonio. 4to. iv and 168 leaves.

453. PAVLI Manvtii in Orationem Ciceronis pro P. Sextio Commentarius. 8vo. 148 leaves.

454. TRE libri di Lettere volgari di Paolo Manvtio. 8vo. 136 leaves.

Editio princeps.

455. ATHENAGORA. 4to. 60 leaves.

456. CAROLI Sigonii Fasti consvlares. Folio. 186 leaves.

457. GAVINI Sambigvcii in Herma-
thenam Bocchianam Interpretatio.   4to.

458. MICHAELIS Thomae Orationes
dvae civiles.   4to. . 82 leaves.

The imprint of these last two works is

Bononiæ apud Antonium Manutium Aldi filium.

Antonio was a bookseller at Bologna, and the
few works he published were undoubtedly printed
by his brother at Venice.

459. PIANTO della Marchesa di Pescara.   8vo.   28 leaves.

460. BERNARDINI Tomitani Cloni-
cvs.   8vo.   12 leaves.

461. BERNARDINI Tomitani Cori-
don.   8vo.   20 leaves.

These last two works were published in one
volume.   Very rare.

462. COMMENTARII di Gaio Givlio
Cesare.   8vo.

In 1556, Frederick Badoaro, a leading senator
of Venice, formed the *Academia Veneziana* con-
sisting of about 100 literary men.   To this Academy
was added a press of which Manutius was made
director.   A catalogue was issued in Italian and
Latin of intended publications.   Only a few works
were issued in 1558-59, all magnificently printed
and now excessively rare.   A list will be found

after the catalogue of the works produced by Aldus the younger, in vol. iii. The plan was, however, a failure, Badoaro having got into disgrace, and been imprisoned in 1562.

M. D. LVII.

463. CAROLI Sigonii Emendationvm libri dvo.   4to.   xii and 160 leaves.

464. SALLVSTIVS.   8vo.

465. DISCORSO di Rinaldo Odoni. 4to.   40 leaves.

This Odoni was the brother-in-law of Manutius.

466. DE gli Elementi.   4to.   34 leaves.

467. ANTIQVITATVM Romanarvm Pauli Manutii liber.   Folio.   iv and 82 leaves.

There are two editions under the same date, the only difference being that the first has only 5 lines on folio 80, whilst the second has 33.

468. IN Epistolas Ciceronis ad Atticvm, Pavli Manvtii Commentarivs.   8vo.   iv. and 432 leaves.

469. COMMENTARIVS Pavli Manvtii in Epistolas M. Tvllii Ciceronis.   8vo. x and 144 leaves.

470. L'EPISTOLE di Cicerone ad Attico.   8vo.

A reprint of the edition of 1555.

471. CONSTANTINI Lascaris Byzantini Grammaticae Compendivm. 8vo. 464 leaves.

A handsome edition.

472. VRBANI Bolzanii Grammaticæ Institvtiones. 8vo. 322 leaves.

473. SONETTI morali di Pietro Massolo. 8vo.

474. CINQVE Orationi di Demosthene. 8vo. 255 leaves.

475. HIERONYMI Faleti de bello Sicambrico. 4to. viii and 138 leaves.

A fine and rare edition.

476. THOMAE Linacri Britanni, De emendata structura Latini sermonis. 8vo. 232 leaves.

The book begins at folio 2.

477. PIANTO della Marchesa di Pescara. 8vo.

A reprint of the previous edition.

478. ANTONIO Castellani Stanze. 4to. 12 pages.

Excessively rare.

479. IACOBI Grifoli Lucinianensis Orationes. 4to. 148 leaves.

M. D. LVIII.

480. ALDI Manvtii Pii Romani grammaticarum institutionum libri iiii. 8vo. 218 leaves.

481. M. TVLLII Ciceronis Epistolae ad Atticvm. 8vo. iv and 348 leaves.

482. BERNARDINI Lavredani in M. Tvllii Ciceronis Orationes. 4to. 300 leaves.

483. CATVLLVS, etc. 8vo. 302 leaves.

484. TERENTIVS. 8vo. xvi and 192 leaves.

The title page is dated 1558 and the colophon 1559.

485. ARCHIMEDIS Opera. Folio. 126 leaves.

486. VIRGILIVS Maro. 8vo. 244 leaves.

Very rare.

487. PTOLEMAEI Planisphaerivm. 4to. 70 leaves.

488. PAULI Aeginetae Opera. 8vo.

A copy is in the library at the Hague.

489. ORATIONES xii. Hieronymi Faleti. Folio. 110 leaves.

490. DEI Commentarj del viaggio in Persia di M. Caterino Zeno. 8vo.

491. AVGVSTARVM imagines. 4to. 216 pages in all.

Very rare.

492. DE tenvis hvmoris febrem. 8vo. xvi. and 268 leaves.

493. ELEGANZE della lingva toscana e latina. 8vo. 192 leaves.

Renouard states that there are two editions under this date, but on what authority I know not.

494. BERNARDINI Georgii Patricii Veneti Epitaphia et Epigrammata aliquot. 4to.

Some copies have no date.

495. AMBROSII Calepini Diction- arivm. Folio. Part i., 232 leaves; part ii., 256 leaves.

The best of the various Aldine editions.

M. D. LIX.

496. ANTIQVITATVM Romanarvm Pauli Manutii Liber. 8vo. 204 leaves.

497. ELEGANZE. 8vo. viii and 184 leaves.

498. CICERONIS opera Rhetorica. 2 vols., 8vo.

A reprint of the edition of 1554.

499. CICERONIS Orationes.   3 vols.,
8vo.

A reprint of the edition of 1554.

500. PAVLI Manvtii in Orationem
Ciceronis pro P. Sextio commentarius.
8vo.   168 leaves.

501. LE Epistole famigliari di Cicerone.
8vo.   380 leaves.

502. CICERONIS de Officiis Libri
iii.   8vo.   148 leaves.

503. HOC volvmine continentur, Commentariorvm de bello Gallico, etc.   8vo.
xvi and 320 leaves.

504. HORATIVS.   8vo.
A reprint of the edition of 1555.

505. C. PLINII Secundi Natvralis
historiae libri triginta septem.   Folio.
xxviii and 484 pages ;—132 pages of index
with separate title page.

506. IVNIORIS Lvdovici Pariseti de
divina benevolentia.   8vo.
A reprint of the edition of 1552.

507. MARCI Antonii Nattae Astensis
de Deo libri xv.   Folio.   iv and 166 leaves.

508. GLI egregi fatti del gran Re
Meliadus.   8vo.

The title-page is dated 1559, but the colophon 1558. Very rare.

509. LA seconda parte delle prodezze ed aspre guerre del gran Meliadus. 8vo.
Very rare.

M. D. LX.

510. CICERONIS Opera philosophica. 2 vols. 8vo.   Vol. i., 332 leaves ; vol. ii., 292 leaves.

511. C. SALLVSTII Crispi de coniuratione Catilinae. 8vo.   viii and 136 leaves.

512. P. VIRGILIVS Maro.   8vo.
A reprint of the edition of 1558.

513. VRBANI Bolzanii Bellvnensis grammaticae institutiones.   8vo.   322 leaves, the last three being wrongly numbered.

514. TERENTIVS. 8vo.   xvi and 200 leaves.

515. ORATIONES septem Caroli Sigonii.   4to.   52 leaves.

516. PACIS Scala. 4to.

517. DIONYSII Halicarnassei de Thvcydidis historia ivdicivm. 4to. 94 leaves.

518. EPISTOLARVM Pavli Manvtii. 8vo. viii and 232 leaves.

519. LETTERE volgari di M. Paolo Manvtio. 8vo. 168 leaves.

520. M. TVLLII Ciceronis Epistolae familiares. 8vo. 368 leaves.

521. OCTAVIANI de Disciplina Encyclio. 4to. iv and 24 leaves.

522. EX libris xxiii Commentariorum in vetera Imperatorum Romanorum numismata Aeneae Vici Liber primus. 4to.

M. D. LXI.

523. ALDI Pii Manvtii Romani Institv tionvm grammaticarvm libri iv. 8vo.

524. ORTHOGRAPHIAE Ratio. 8vo. 56 leaves.

525. CICERO de Officiis. 8vo. 163 leaves.

526. M. TVLLII Ciceronis Epistolae ad Atticvm. 8vo. 408 leaves.

527. COMMENTARIVS Pavli Manvtii in Epistolas Ciceronis ad Atticvm. 8vo. 438 leaves.

528. IN omnes de Arte Rhetorica Ciceronis libros Commentaria, etc. Folio.

A reprint of the edition of 1546. .

529. HORATIVS. 8vo. viii and 184 leaves.

530. IO. Baptistae Pignae Oratio. 4to.

531. EPISTOLARVM Pavli Manvtii libri v. 8vo. xvi and 240 leaves.

532. HIERONYMVS Gabvcinivs de Morbo Comitiali. 4to.

533. DE Ordine ac Methodo in Scientia servandis. 4to. 32 leaves.

534. ORATIONES duæ, altera Iacobi Sadoleti ad Carolum v. Altera I. Bapt. Compegii de tuenda religione. 4to.

535. C. IULII Caesaris Commentarii. 8vo.

A reprint of the edition of 1559.

536. ELEGANZE. 8vo.

A reprint of the edition of 1559.

In 1561 Pius IV. wrote to Manutius begging him to come to Rome and superintend the printing of various works of theology. After some hesitation he accepted the offers made him, and in August left Venice, and was received at Rome with great honour. His family, whom he had left behind, soon joined him, and for nine years he printed a number of now rare works in the Empire City. Meanwhile, the Venice press was not idle, and was shortly placed under the management of his son Aldus the Younger. In a few years, however, Manutius finding himself no longer treated with the same generosity and attention as at first, began to long to return to Venice. This he did in September 1570. To distinguish the works printed at Rome from those printed at Venice, I have marked the former with a *.

M. D. LXII.

537. CICERONIS Orationes. 3 vols. 8vo. Vol. i., 348 leaves; vol. ii., 312 leaves; vol. iii. 296 leaves.

538. M. TVLLII Ciceronis Epistolae familiares. 8vo.

A reprint of the edition of 1560.

539. IN Epistolas M. Tvllii Ciceronis ad M. Ivnivm Brvtvm et ad Q. Ciceronem fratrem, Pauli Manutii commentarius. 8vo.

A reprint of the edition of 1557.

540. CICERONIS Opera philosophica. 2 vols. 8vo.

A reprint of the edition of 1560.

541. CATVLLVS. 8vo. 302 leaves.

542. EX libris xxii Commentariorvm in vetera Imperatorvm Romanorvm nvmismata Aeneae Vici Liber primvs. 4to.

543. L'ARTE del predicare. 8vo. 120 leaves.

This book bears the name of Andrea Torresano, grandson of Andrea d'Asola.

*544. DE Concilio liber Reginaldi Poli Cardinalis. 4to. viii and 64 leaves.

The first vol. printed by Manutius at Rome. Rare.

*545. REFORMATIO Angliae ex decretis Reginaldi Poli Cardinalis. 4to. 28 leaves.

Rare.

*546. SANCTI Ioannis Chrysostomi de Virginitate liber. 4to. viii and 64 leaves.

*547. GREGORII Nyseni liber de Virginitate. 4to. viii and 90 pages; 1 blank leaf.

*548. DE Virginitate. 4to. 116 leaves.

*549. DIVI Thomae Aqvinatis in librum B. Iob expositio. 4to.

*550. CLAVDII Ptolemaei liber de Analemmate. 4to. iv and 96 leaves.

*551. MATTHAEI Cvrtii Papiensis de Prandii ac Caenae modo libellus. 4to. iii and 90 leaves.

*552. MARIANI Victorii de Sacramento Confessionis liber. 8vo.

*553. THEODORETI in visiones Danielis prophetae Commentarivs. Folio. viii and 156 pages.

*554. ANTONII Bernardi Institutio in Logicam. 4to.

555. M. A. NATTAE de libris suis. Folio.

M. D. LXIII.

*556. BEATI Theodoriti, in Canticvm canticorvm Explanatio. Folio. iv and 68 leaves.

557. Le Epistole famigliari di Cicerone. 8vo.

A reprint of 1559 edition.

558. CICERONIS Epistolae ad Atticvm. 8vo. 408 leaves.

559. ASCONII Pediani Explanatio in Ciceronis Orationes. 8vo. xii and 104 leaves.

560. C. SALLVSTII Crispi Conivratio Catilinae. 8vo. xii and 172 leaves.

Some copies bear the imprint of Rome.

561. P. VIRGILIVS Maro. 8vo.

Reprint of 1558 edition.

*562. DIVI Caecilii Cypriani Opera. Folio. xxviii and 476 pages.

* 563. GREGORII Nyseni Conciones qvinque de Oratione Domini. 4to. xx and 168 pages.

* 564. FRANCISCI Vargas De Episcoporum iurisdictione. 4to. xvi and 160 pages.

565. ELEGANZE. 8vo.

566. TERENTIVS. 8vo. 216 leaves.

567. ISOTAE Nogorolae, Dialogvs. 4to. 37 leaves.

M. D. LXIV.

568. ALDI Manvtii Grammaticarum institutionum libri iiii. 8vo. 218 leaves.

569. CICERONIS opera Rhetorica. 2 vols., 8vo. Vol i., 198 leaves; vol. ii., 298 leaves.

570. CICERONIS Epistolae ad Atticum. 8vo. 308 leaves.

571. CICERO de Officiis, etc. 8vo.

572. HORATIUS. 8vo. 200 leaves.

573. LETTERE volgari. 3 vols., 8vo. Vol i., 144 leaves; vol. ii., 130 leaves; vol. iii., 220 leaves.

574. C. IULII Caesaris Commentari-

orvm De Bello Gallico, libri viii. 8vo. 380 leaves.

575. M. ANTONII Flaminii Psalmorvm explanatio. 8vo. 360 leaves.

576. M. ANTONII Nattae Opera. Folio. 130 leaves.

577. AMBROSII Calepini Dictionarium, etc. Folio. 428 leaves.

578. VAL. Palermi Orationes duæ simulque Pastorale Carmen, quibus funera trium fratrum Nogarolarum Comitum Veronensium deflentur. 4to.

*579. CANONES, et Decreta sacrosancti oecvmenici, et generalis Concilii Tridentini svb Pavlo iii, Ivlio iii, Pio iiii, Pontificibvs Max. *Romæ, Apud Paulum Manutium, Aldi F. m. d. lxiiii. Cum priuilegio. Pii iiii. Pont. Max.* Folio. 239 pages.

Extremely rare.

*580. *The same*, 4to, 284 pages.

*581. *The same*, 8vo, 336 leaves.

582. *The same*, 8vo, 186 leaves.

583. *The same*, 4to, 142 leaves.

*584. CANONES, et Decreta sacrosancti oecumenici, et generalis Concilii Tridentini sub Paulo iii, Iulio iii, Pio iiii,

Pontificibvs Max. Index Dogmatum, &
Reformationis. — *Romae apud Paulum
Manutium, Aldi F. m. d. lxiiii. In
Aedibus Populi Romani.* Folio. 250 pages.

* 585. *The same,* 382 pages.

586. *The same,* 8vo, 231 leaves.

* 587. *The same, Romæ m.d. lxiv.* Folio.
May be distinguished from the others by its
having the Bull of Pius IV. before the Index.

588. *The same,* 8vo, 392 pages.

* 589. SALUIANI, de vero Ivdicio et
Providentia Dei libri viii. Folio. 433
pages.

* 590. DIUI Evcherii Commentarii.
Folio. viii and 391 pages.

* 591. BREUIARIUM Romanvm.
Folio.

* 592. INDEX librorvm prohibitorvm.
4to.
Very rare.

———

M. D. LXV.

593. CANONES et Decreta Concilii
Tridentini. 8vo. xxiv and 184 leaves.

594. CICERONIS Opera philosophica.
2 vols. 8vo. Vol. i., 328 leaves ; vol. ii.,
295 leaves.

595. ELEGANZE. 8vo.

596. JACOBI Taurelli Patronymia. 4to.

597. PETRI Bizzari varia Opvscula. 8vo. 156 leaves.

Rare.

*598. STANISLAI Hosii Confessio Catholicæ fidei. Folio.

*599. EPISTOLAE D. Hieronymi Stridoniensis. 3 vols. Folio.

*600. ANGELOMI Annotationes in libros Regum. Folio. 336 pages.

*601. LA Congiura de' Baroni del Regno di Napoli contra il Re Ferdinando i. da Camillo Persio. 4to.

M. D. LXVI.

602. C. IULII. Caesaris Commentariorum. 8vo. 376 leaves.

693. ORTHOGRAPHIAE Ratio ab. Aldo Manvtio Collecta. 8vo. 1007 pages.

604. L'EPISTOLE famigliari di Cicerone, etc. 8vo.

605. CATULLUS. 8vo. 419 pages; 1 leaf for anchor; 1 blank leaf.

606. Q. HORATIUS Flaccvs. 4to. Part i., 262 leaves; part ii., 220 leaves.

607. HORATIUS. 8vo.

A reprint of the 1564 edition.

608. T. LIUII Patavini, Historia. Folio. 559 leaves in all.

609. TERENTIUS. 8vo. 216 leaves.

610. VRBANI Bolzanii Bellvnensis Grammaticae Institvtiones ad Graecam Lingvam, etc. 8vo. 322 leaves.

611. CONSTITVTIONES et Decreta. 8vo. xvi and 294 pages.

*612. CATECHISMUS. Folio. iv and 371 pages.

*613. CATECHISMUS, etc. 8vo. viii and 684 pages;—2 blank leaves.

*614. CATECHISMUS, etc. 4to.

*615. EPISTOLAE D. Hieronymi. 3 vols. 8vo. Vol. i., 72 and 450 pages; vol. ii., pages 451 to 1179; vol. iii., 672 pages.

*616. MARIANI Victorii de Sacramento Confessionis. 8vo.

617. CANONES et Decreta. 8vo.

618. MATTHAEI Curtii de Prandii. 8vo.

E

M. D. LXVII.

619. M. TULLII Ciceronis Epistolae ad Atticvm, ad Brvtvm, ad Qvinctvm fratrem, cum correctionibus Pauli Manutij. 8vo. 408 leaves.

620. M. TULLII Ciceronis Epistolae familiares. 8vo. 372 leaves.

621. CICERONIS de Officiis. 8vo. 168 leaves.

622. TIBULLUS. 8vo. 380 leaves.

*623. CATECHISMO. 8vo. 638 pages; 1 blank leaf.

624. CATECHISMO, &c. 4to. viii and 536 pages.

625. C. SALLUSTII. Crispi Conivratio. 8vo. 216 leaves.

*626 CATECHISMUS. 8vo. viii and 686 pages; 1 blank leaf.

627. LETTERE volgari, 3 vols. 8vo.

.*628. LUCÆ Pæti. I. C. de ivdiciaria form. 8vo. viii and 571 pages; 2 blank leaves.

629. L'ARCHITETTURA di Pietro Cataneo. Folio.

M. D. LXVIII.

630. CANONES et Decreta S. Concilii Tridentini, &c. 8vo.

631. CATECHISMO. 8vo. xxxii and 608 pages.

632. BREUIARIUM Romanvm, &c. Folio.

633. COMMENTARIUS Pavli. Manvtii in. Epistolas. Ciceronis ad. Atticvm. 8vo. 805 pages.

634. ALDI Manutii Grammaticae Institutiones. 8vo.

M. D. LXIX.

635. RHETORICORUM ad. C. Herennivm libri. iv. 8vo. 400 pages.

636. CICERONIS De Oratore. 8vo. 591 pages.

637. M. TULLII. Ciceronis Orationvm partes iii. 3 vols., 8vo. Vol. i., 703 pages; vol. ii., 629 pages, 1 blank leaf; vol. iii., 621 pages, 1 blank leaf.

638. L'Epistole di Cicerone ad Attico. 8vo.

639. Antiqvitatvm Romanarvm Pavli. Manvtii liber. 8vo. 367 pages.

640. RIME del Commendatore Annibal Caro. 4to. viii and 107 pages.

641. DUE Orationi di Gregorio Nazanzeno 4to. viii and 148 pages.

642. CANONES et Decreta SS. Concilii Tridentini, etc. 8vo. 216 leaves.

643. ORATIONES Responsa Literae. 8vo. viii and 189 pages;—2 blank leaves.

Undoubtedly printed at the Aldine Press, though bearing the name of D. de Farris.

*644. CATECHISMUS. 8vó. viii and 670 pages.

645. CATECHISMO. 8vo.

646. P. MANUTII Epistolarum Libri viii. 8vo.

647. C. IULII Cæsar. 8vo. xii and 399 pages.

648. RHETORICORUM ad C. Herennivm libri iiii. 8vo.

649. CICERONIS de Oratore libri iii. 8vo. 288 pages.

———

M. D. LXX.

650. CICERONIS Officiorvm libri tres. 8vo. 56 leaves.

651. CICERONIS Epistolae ad Atticvm. 8vo. 400 leaves.

652. CICERONIS Epistolae ad. Atticvm. 8vo. 816 pages.

653. MARII Nizolii Thesaurus Ciceronianus. Folio.

654. COMMENTARIA in Epistolas Ciceronis ad Atticum. 8vo. 437 leaves.

655. ELEGANZE. 8vo. 265 pages; —1 blank leaf.

656. EPITHETA M. T. Ciceronis collecta a. P. Ioanne. Nvnnesio Valentino. 8vo.

657. NICOLAI Clenardi Institvtiones lingvae. Graecae. 8vo.

658. MARCI Antonii Nattae de Deo libri xv. Folio.

659. NICCOLO Guidani. Eustachia, Commedia. 8vo.

660. CICERONIS Oraticnvm partes iii. 3 vols., 8vo.

661. HORATIUS. 8vo. 188 leaves.

662. P. TERENTII Afri Comoediae sex. 8vo. 251 leaves.

663. TERENTIUS. 8vo. 224 leaves.

664. IACOBI Sannazarii opera omnia. 8vo. 104 leaves.

665. BRUTI Epistolæ. 8vo.

666. C. J. CAESARIS Commentarii, etc. 8vo.

_____

M. D. LXXI.
667. AUTHORITATES sacrae scriptvrae. 4 vols., 4to.

668. DE sacrosancto Missae Sacram. 4to.

669. PAULI de Palacio Enarrationes. 2 vols., 8vo.   Vol. i., 400 leaves;—vol. ii., 376 leaves.

670. CATECHISMO. 8vo.

671. CICERONIS Epistolae familiares. dictae Scholia Pauli Manutij, nuper aucta. 8vo.

672. C. VELLEII Patercvli Historiae. 8vo.   180 pages.

673. C. IULII. Caesaris Commenta riorvm De Bello Gallico, libri iix.   8vo.

674. EPISTOLARUM Pavli. Manvtii libri. x.   8vo.

675. DE Gentib. et Familiis Romanorum.   4to.

Henceforth the publications of the Aldine Press have little to interest.

_____

M. D. LXXII.
676. CICERONIS Epistolae ad fami-

liares, &c.   8vo.   870 pages;   1 . blank leaf.

677. Ciceronis Orationes in M. Antonium. 8vo.

678. RIME del Commendatore Annibal Caro. 4to. 120 pages.

679. DE le Lettere familiari del Commendatore Annibal Caro volvme primo. 4to.

680. RAPHAELIS Cyllenii Angeli Orationes. 8vo.

681. T. LIUII Patavini Historia. Folio.

682. HIERONYMI Rubei Historia Ravennatensis. Folio.

683. DISCORSO intorno all' Eccellenza delle Repubbliche. 4to.

684. OFFICUM B. Mariæ Virginis. 24mo.

M. D. LXXIII.

685. LUCAL Paeti De Mensvris et Ponderibvs Romanis et Graecis. Folio. 48 leaves.

686. C. CRISPI Sallvstii Historiae. 8vo.

687. EPISTOLARUM Pavli. Manvtii. Libri. xi. 8vo. 360 leaves.

688. LE Epistole famigliari di Cicerone. 8vo. 406 leaves.

689. CATECHISMO secondo il Concilio di Trento, &c. 8vo.

M. D. LXXIV.

690. DE le Letterre familiari del Commendatore Annibal Caro volvme primo. 4to. xii and 296 pages.

691. CANONES et Decreta Concilii Tridentini, etc. 8vo.

692. MANUTII Scholia in Cicer. Ep. ad fam. 8vo.

693. MISSALE Romanvm. 4to.

On the 6th of April 1574, Paulus Manutius died, at the age of 61. He was buried in the Dominican Church at Rome. He had fought a noble fight, and he descended into the grave amidst the tears of his family and friends, and the universal regret of all. He was a master indeed in the Art of typography; the finest Latin scholar, to judge from his letters, of his age; a dutiful son, an affectionate father, and a true and noble man.

END OF VOL. II.

The Aldine Press.

Bibliotheca Curiosa.

A BIBLIOGRAPHICAL SKETCH

OF

THE ALDINE PRESS

AT VENICE,

FORMING

A CATALOGUE

*Of all Works issued by Aldus and his successors,
from 1494 to 1597, and a list of all known
Forgeries or Imitations,*

TRANSLATED AND ABRIDGED FROM

ANT. AUG. RENOUARD'S

"*Annales de L'Imprimerie des Aldes,*"

AND

REVISED AND CORRECTED

BY

EDMUND GOLDSMID, F.R.H.S., F.S.A.(Scot.)

IN THREE VOLUMES.

VOL. III.

ALDUS THE YOUNGER, ETC.

PRIVATELY PRINTED, EDINBURGH.

—

1887.

THE ALDINE PRESS.

ALDUS THE YOUNGER.

LDUS the Younger was the son of Paulus Manutius, and was born on the 13th February, 1547. When aged 11, a work was published under his name, *Eleganze della lingua Latina e toscana*, probably written by his father. During his father's long stay at Rome, Aldus was appointed to manage the Venice press. In 1572 Aldus married Francesca Lucrezia, of the Giunti family, of Florence, and two years later his father's death left him sole master of the printing establishment. In 1585 he accepted the chair of Rhetoric at Bologna. Thence he passed to Pisa in 1587, and to Rome the following year, where the same chair had been

placed at his disposal three years before. In
1590 he obtained the management of the Vatican
Press. Meanwhile the Aldine Press at Venice
was not idle, but, with Nicolo Manassi as manager,
continued to produce edition after edition. I do
not agree with Renouard's view that Manassi was
the *owner*, not the *manager*, of the works. On
the 28th of October 1797, Aldus died at Rome, at
the age of 50.

To his grandfather and father he owed the
celebrity he enjoyed, far more than to his own
merits. Anxious to make a name as an *author*,
he neglected the duties of a *printer*, and the works
printed by him never have had, and never will
have, the value of those printed by Aldus the
Elder and Paulus Manutius. Consequently, I
have not thought it necessary to go into so many
details as to his productions as I have done with
regard to those of his father and grandfather.
With a few exceptions, Aldine editions after 1574
are little sought after. In Aldus Manutius the
Younger ended a family, the honour of literature
and typography, whose fame cannot die so long
as a single one of the volumes printed. by them
during a whole century shall continue to exist !   -

M. D. LXXV.

692. Aldi. Pii. Manvtii Grammati-

carvm Institutionvm libri. iv. 8vo. 431
pages.

693. Eleganze. 8vo. 415 pages.

694. Epitome Orthographiae Aldi
Manvtii. 8vo. 144 leaves.

695. M. T. Ciceronis Epistolae familiares. 8vo.

696. Locvtioni dell' Epistole di Cicerone.
8vo. 469 pages.

697. Octaviani Ferrarii Hieronymi. De
Sermonibus Exotericis Liber. 4to. 120
pages ;—1 blank leaf.

698. M. Antonii Mureti Orationes xxiii.
8vo. xvi and 220 leaves ;—1 blank leaf.

699. C. Ivlii Caesaris Commentarii.
8vo. ccc and 897 pages.

700. De le Lettere familiari del Commendatore Annibal Caro. Volvme
secondo. 4to. 458 pages.

701. Canones et Decreta SS. Concilii
Tridentini, etc. 8vo.

702. Catechismvs Concilii Tridentini,
etc. 8vo.

703. Catechismo ai Parrochi. 8vo.

704. Vita dell' Imperator Carlo v. 4to.
352 leaves.

705. Hercvlis. Ciofani in P. Ovidii. Metamorphosin ex xvii. antiqvis libris Obseruationes. 8vo. xliv and 223 pages.

706. P. Terentivs Afer. 8vo. xlviii and 446 pages.

M. D. LXXVI.

707. Aldi Pii Manvtii Grammaticae Institvtiones, etc. 8vo.

708. De Qvaesitis. 8vo.

709. Aldvs Manvtivs de Toga et Tvnica Romanorvm. 8vo.

710. Bvcolica. Georgica. Aeneis. 8vo.

711. Mvreti Orationes et Hymni. 8vo.

712. C. Jvlii Caesaris Commentarii. 8vo.

713. Del Tevere di M. Andrea Bacci. 4to. viii and 320 pages.

714. In Q. Horatii. Commentarius. 4to. xvi and 125 pages ;—1 blank leaf. -

715. D'Antonio Persio Trattato dell' Ingegno dell' hvomo. 8vo. 75 leaves.

716. Marii Nizolii Thesaurus Ciceronianus. Folio.

717. Osservationi intorno alle bellezze della lingva latina Di F. Angelo Rocca da

Camerino.   8vo.   xxxii and 458 pages ;—
1 blank leaf.

718. Pauli Clarantis Epitome.   4to.

719. Ambr.   Calepini   Dictionarium.
Folio.

M. D. LXVII.

720. Apophthegmatvm ex. optimis vtrivsqve. lingvae scriptoribvs libri. iix. 12mo.
706 pages followed by 24 leaves.

721. Sallvstivs.   8vo.

M. D. LXXVIII.

722. In M. Tvllii Ciceronis Orationes
Paulli   Manutij   Commentarius.   Folio.
Vol. i.   iv and 356 pages.

723. Gaspari   Contareni   Cardinalis
Opera.   Folio.

724. F. Cornelio Bellanda di Verona
de' Minori.   Viaggio spirituale.   4to.

725. Gabriels Flammae Oratio.   4to.

M. D. LXXIX.

726. In M. Tvllii Ciceronis Orationvm
volvmen secvndvm et tertivm Paulli
Manutii Commentarius.   Vol. ii., 370
pages ; vol. iii., 458 pages.

727. M. Tvllii Ciceronis Epistolae familiares. Folio.

728. B. Lorenzo Givstiniano Del dispregio del Mondo. 4to.

M. D. LXXX.

729. Virgilivs. 8vo.

730. Epistolarvm Pavlli Manvtii libri xii. 8vo.

731. Eleganze. 8vo.

732. Herculis Ciofani Scholia in Ovidii Halieuticon. 8vo.

M. D. LXXXI.

733. Censorini de die. natali liber. 8vo.

734. Antiqvitatvm Romanarvm Pavlli. Mannvccii liber de. Senatv. 4to.

735. De Natvra Daemonvm libri iiii. Io. Lavrentii Ananiae Tabernatis. 8vo.

736. De Vitis Sanctorvm ab Aloysio Lipomano. 6 vols., Folio. Rare.

737. Philippi Mocenici Vniuersales Institutiones. Folio.

738. L'Agicóltvra. 4to.

739. Aminta favola boscareccia di M.

Torqvato Tasso,   8vo.   viii and 70 pages,
1 blank leaf.

Editio princeps.   Very rare.

740. Rime e Prose di Torqvato Tasso.
8vo.

741. In M. Tvllii Ciceronis de. Officiis
Comm.   Folio.

M. D. LXXXII.

742. Pavlli Manvtii in M. T. Ciceronis
Epistolas Commentarivm.   Folio.

743. Locvtioni dell' Epistole di
Cicerone.   8vo.

744. Lettere facete e piacevoli.   8vo.

745. Essame de gl'Ingegni de gli
hvomini.   8vo.   xvi and 367 pages.

746. Catechismvs.   8vo.

747. Catechismo.   8vo.

748. Delle Rime del Signor Torqvato
Tasso parte prima e seconda.   2 vols.
12mo.

749. Gli Straccioni, Commedia di
Annibal Caro.   12mo.

M. D. LXXXIII.

750. Aldi Manvtii Ivnioris in M. T.

Ciceronis de Rhetorica volvmen primvm et secvndvm Commentarius. Folio.

751. Aldi Manutii Ivnioris in M. T. Ciceronis de Philosophia volvmen primvm et secvndvm Commentarivs. 2 vols. Folio.

752. M. Tvllivs Cicero Mannvcciorvm Commentariis illvstratvs antiquaeq, lectioni restitutus.—*Venetiis Apud Aldum. m. d. lxxxiii.* 10 vols. Folio.

753. Germani Avdeberti Avrelii Venetiæ. 4to.

754. Delle Rime del Signor T. Tasso. 2 vols. 12mo.

M. D. LXXXIV.

755. Il perfetto Gentil'hvomo. 4to.

756. Qvaestionvm grammaticarvm Libri. iix. 8vo.

757. Strigilis Grammatica. 8vo.

M. D. LXXXV.

758. Locvtioni di Terentio. 8vo.

759. P. Virgilii Maronis Opera. 8vo.

760. Calestri, Tragedia di Carlo Turco Asolano. 8vo.

761. Agnelle, Commedia di Carlo Turco Asolano. 8vo.

762. Della nvova Disciplina. Folio. 200 pages.

763. Aggivnta alle Rime, et Prose del Sig. Torqvato Tasso. 12mo.

764. La Vicissitudine ò mvtabile varietà delle cose. 4to.

765. Vita di Cosimo de' Medici. Folio.

766. Scipii Gentilis Solymeidos libri duo priores. 4to.

C'est la traduction en vers hexamètres latins, des deux premiers livres de la *Gerusalemme liberata*, qui avaient été déjà imprimés à Lyon, *apud Joan. Albuseum* 1584, in-4to.—*Renouard.*

M. D. LXXXVI.

767. Essame de gl'Ingegni. 8vo.

768. Declaratio difficilium terminorum Theologiae. 8vo.

769. Eleganze. 12mo.

770. Vita di Cosimo de' Medici. Folio.

771. De Lavdibvs Vitae. 4to.

M. D. LXXXVII.

772. Officivm B. Mariae Virginis. 12mo.

773. Locvtioni dell' Epistole di Cicerone. 12mo.

774. Constitvtiones et Privilegia Patriarchatus et Cleri Venetiarum. 4to.

775. Demonomania de gli Stregoni. 4to.

M. D. LXXXVIII.

776. Medicvs Hebraevs defensvs. 4to.

777. Heroidvm Epistolae P. Ouidii Nasonis, &c. 8vo.

778. C. Sallvstii Crispi Conivratio Catilinae. 8vo.

779. C. Ivlii Caesaris Commentarii. 8vo.

780. Lepidi Comici Veteris Philodoxios. 8vo.

M. D. LXXXIX.

781. Annibal Caro. Commedia detta gli Straccioni. 12mo.

782. Concilivm Tridentinum. 8vo.

783. Gaspari Contareni de Republica, 8vo.

784. Demonomania di Giov. Bodino &c.   4to.

785. De Natvra Daemonvm.   8vo.

786. Rime amorose e pastorali.   4to.

787. Aminta favola Boschereccia di Torqvato Tasso.   12mo.

788. De Fascino libri tres.   8vo.

789. Discorsi della Penitenza.   8vo.

790. Orthographia Manutiana in tauole.

791. Governo della famiglia.   8vo.

792. I libri di Gio. Mesve de i Semplici pvrgativi.   8vo.

———— ——

M. D. XC.

793. Aldi Manvtii Paulli F. Epitome Orthographiae.   8vo.

794. Osservationi intorno alle bellezze della lingua latina.   8vo.

795. Discorso di Cosmographia in dialogo.   8vo.

796. Jacobi Pontani Progymnasmata. 8vo.

797. Inscriptiones antiqvae Avgvstae Vindelicorvm.   4to.

798. Oracoli Politici. 8vo.

799. Pavlli Manvtii Epistolarum libri xii. 8vo.

800. Essame de gl' Ingegni de gl' hvomini. 8vo.

801. Aminta del Sig. Torqvato Tasso. 4to. viii and 80 pages.

802. Biblia sacra vvlgatae editionis tribvs tomis distincta. *Romae, ex Typographia Apostolica Vaticana. M. d. xc.* Folio. xxii and 1141 pages, besides two leaves before folio 480, and two before the New Testament.

Extremely rare, having been suppressed by Gregory xiv. for incorrectness.

——— ———

M. D. XCI.

803. Aldi Manvtii Iunioris Orthographiae Ratio. 8vo.

804. De Gentib. et familiis Romanorvm. 8vo.

805. Agricoltvra. 4to.

806. Della Repvblica et Magistrati di Venetia libri v. 8vo. 384 pages.

807. Fragmenta Tabvlae antiquae. 4to.

Very rare.

808. Conversio et Passio SS. Martyrum Afrae, Hilariae, etc. 4to. 68 leaves.

809. Dello Stato delle Repvbliche. 4to.

810. F. Cornelio Bellanda Viaggio spirituale. 8vo.

M. D. XCII.

811. M. T. Ciceronis de Officiis libri tres, etc. 8vo.

812. T. Liuij Patauini Historiarvm libri. Folio.

813. Demonomania di Giov. Bodino. 4to.

814. Della Vicissitvdine ò mvtabile varietà delle cose. 4to.

815. Pavlli Manvtii Antiquitatum Romanorum libri iv. 8vo.

816. Biblia sacra vvlgatae editionis. Folio.

M. D. XCIV.

817. Locvtioni dell'Epistole de Cicerone. 8vo.

818. Eleganze. 8vo.

819. Marci. Velseri Matthaei F. Ant. N Patricii. Avg. Vind Rervm Avgvstanär. Vindelicar Libri. octo. Folio

· M. D. XCV.

820. Della Origine et Svccessi de gli Slavi. 4to.

821. Discorso di Cosmografia in dialogo. 8vo.

M. D. XCVI.

822. Oratio de Virtutibus D. N. Iesu Christi in ejus passione ostensis, Romae ad Alex. vi. P. M. in Parasceve habita. *Romae, ex Typographia Dominici Basae.*

M. D. XCVII.

823. Del dispreggio del mondo e delle sue vanità. 4to.

PUBLICATIONS OF THE ACADEMIA VENETA.*

MD. LVIII.

1. Sommario dell' Opere, che ha da mandare in luce l'Accademia Venetiana. Folio.

Very rare.

2. Svmma Librorvm, qvos in lvcem emittet Academia Veneta. 4to. 44 leaves.

Very rare.

3. De Dei Locvtione Marci Antonii Nattae Astensis Oratio. 4to. 26 leaves.

4. (*Leonis Baptistae Alberti*) De Legato Pontificio. 4to. 24 leaves.

5. De Miseria hvmana. 4to. 68 leaves.

6. Syriani antiqvissimi interpretis in ii. xii. et xiii. Aristotelis libros Metaphysices Commentarius. 4to. 136 leaves.

7. Progne, Tragoedia. 4to.

8. Historia delle cose occorse nel regno d'Inghilterra. 8vo.

---

* See vol. ii., page 57.

9. Pavli Manvtii Epistolae, et Praefationes qvae dicvntur. 8vo. 158 leaves.

10. I diece Circoli dell' Imperio. 4to. 44 leaves.

Rare.

11. Discorso intorno alle cose della gverra. 4to. 54 leaves.

Very rare.

12. Le Institvtioni dell' Imperio. 4to. 60 leaves.

Very rare.

———

M. D. LIX.

13. Flavii Alexii Vgonii, De maximis Italiæ atque Græciæ calamitatibus. 4to. 78 leaves.

14. Orationes clarorvm hominvm. 4to. 188 leaves.

Very rare.

15. Federici Delphini de fluxu maris. Folio.

Very rare.

16. In Aristotelis Topica nova Explanatio. Folio.

Very rare.

FORGERIES.

As I have stated (vol. 1, p. 23), no sooner had Aldus introduced his *italic*, than not only imitations (which would of course be allowable), but actual forgeries, bearing the *name* of Aldus, were produced at Venice, Basle, but especially at Lyons. I subjoin a list of these various editions :

1. Virgilius. 8vo. No date, and leaves unnumbered.

2. Ivvenalis. Persivs. 8vo. No date, and leaves unnumbered.

There are two editions, one very incorrect, the other much better.

3. Horativs. 8vo. No date.

4. Lvcanvs. 8vo. Leaves unnumbered.

5. Prvdentivs. Prosper. Ioannes. Damascenus. Cosmus Hierosolymitanus Marcus Episcopus Taluontis Theophanes. 8vo. Leaves unnumbered.

6. Le terze Rime di Dante. 8vo. No date, and leaves unnumbered.

7. Terentivs. 8vo. No date.

8. Martialis. 8vo. No date, and leaves unnumbered.

9. Catvllvs. Tibvllvs. Propetivs.   No date, and leaves unnumbered.

10. Catvllvs. Tibvllvs. Propertivs. 8vo. No date, and leaves unnumbered.

11. Ivstinvs. 8vo. No date.

12. M. T. C. Epistolae familiares. 8vo. No date.

13. Ovidii Opera. 3 vols., 8vo. No date, and leaves unnumbered.

14. Ovidii Opera. 3 vols., 8vo. No date; leaves numbered.

15. Valerii Maximi dictorvm et factorvm memorabilivm libri novem. 8vo.   No date, and leaves unnumbered.

16. Phylostratvs de vita Apollonii Tyanei scriptor lvcvlentvs a Philippo Beroaldo castigatvs. 8vo. No date, and leaves unnumbered.

17. Le Cose vvlgari di Messer Francesco Petrarcha. 8vo. No date, and leaves unnumbered.

18. Le Cose volgari di Messer Francesco Petrarcha. 8vo. No date; leaves numbered.

19. Il Petrarcha. 8vo. No date; leaves numbered.
Probably printed at Venice.

20. Habentvr hoc volvmine haec Theodoro Gaza interprete, etc. 8vo. No date.

21. Xenophon. 8vo. No date, and leaves unnumbered.

22. Salvstivs. 8vo. Dated 1504; leaves unnumbered.

23. Hecvba, et Iphigenia in Aulide Euripidis tragœdiæ. 8vo. No date, and leaves unnumbered.

24. Valerii Maximi dictorvm et factorvm memorabilivm. Libri novum. 8vo. Dated 1508 : leaves numbered.

25. Caii Svetonii Tranquilli de vita. xii. Caesarvm. 8vo. Leaves numbered.

26. C. Ivlivs Caesar, a Phil. Beroaldo. 8vo. Dated 1508.

27. Qvintilianvs. 8vo. Dated 1510; leaves unnumbered.

28. Iustini Historia. 8vo. Dated 1510; leaves unnumbered.

29. C. Plinii secvndi Veronensis Historiæ natvralis. 2 vols., 8vo. Dated 1510; leaves numbered.

30. Valerii Maximi dictorvm et factorvm memorabilivm. Libri novem. 8vo. Dated 1510; leaves numbered.

31. Avli Gellii Noctes Atticae. 8vo. Dated 1512 ; leaves numbered.

32. Silii Italici Opvs. 8vo. Dated 1513; leaves unnumbered.

33. Opera Ioannis Ioviani Pontani.

8vo. Dated 1514; leaves unnumbered.

34. Catvllvs. Tibvllvs. Propertivs. 8vo. Dated 1518; leaves unnumbered.

35. Martialis. 8vo. Dated 1526.

36. Commentaria Caesaris. 8vo. Dated 1519; leaves numbered.

37. Annei Lvcani Poema. 8vo. Dated 1521; leaves numbered.

38. Virgilivs. 8vo. Dated 1521; leaves numbered.

39. M. Vitrvvii de Architectura libri decem. 8vo. Dated 1523; leaves numbered.

40. Flavivs Vegetivs de re militari. 8vo. Dated 1523; leaves numbered.

41. Terentivs noviter impressvs. 8vo Dated 1523.

42. Juuenalis. Persius. 12mo. Dated 1525; leaves numbered.

43. Gaurici Pomponii Elegiæ, Eclogæ, Silvæ, et Epigrammata. 8vo. Dated 1526.

44. Pontani Opera. 2 vols., 8vo. No date; leaves numbered.

45. Strozzii Poetae Pater et filivs. 8vo. No date.

DOUBTFUL EDITIONS.

Aldine editions of the following authors have been announced by various Bibliographers, but of the existence of none of them have I been able to trace the slightest real proof. Many owe their origin to careless compilers, many to a figure scatched out with a penknife, as for instance, in an edition of M.D.I., removing the I and creating an edition of M.D. Again, with a pen, by *adding* a I, the edition has become M.D.II., and so on. All these editions, which I believe have no existence, but which I have found mentioned by Bibliographers, I have collected in the following list :—

1. AEGINETÆ opera. Folio. 1534.
2. ALDI Grammatica Graeca. 1497.
3. AMMONIUS in Pophyrium. 8vo. 1545.
4. ARISTIDIS Orationes. 1527.
5. ARISTOTELES de Animal. Folio. 1503.

6. ARISTOTELIS Mechanica. 1507.
7. ARISTOTELIS Poetica. 8vo. 1556, 1563.
8. AVERROIS questio. Fo. 1497.
9. BEMBO. Gli Asolani. 8vo. 1555.
10. CÆSAR. 8vo. 1565.
11. CALLEPINI dict. Folio. 1559, 1563, 1573, 1575, 1577, 1592.
12. CAMPEGII T. opera. 8vo. 1554.
13. CATULLUS, etc. 8vo. 1511, 1564.
14. CICERO. Rhetorica. 4vo. 1510.
15. CICERO. Epist. ad Atticum. 8vo. 1542, 1553.
16. CICERO. Epist. famil. 8vo. 1545, 1548, 1552, 1572, 1582, 1592.
17. CICERO. De Oratore. 4to. 1553.
18. CICERO. Orationes. 8vo. 1561, 1565.
19. CICERONE Epistole famigliari. 8vo. 1560.
20. COTTÆ J. Carmina. 8vo. 1529.
21. DECLARATIO difficilium terminorum
    . theologiæ. 8vo. 1584.
22. DIALOGHI di Amore. 8vo. 1558.
23. DONATI (H.) Oratio. 8vo. 15)1.
24. ESSAME de gl'Ingegni. 8vo. 1589.
25. GALENUS. 1498.
26. GIUSTINIANO. G. La Eneide. 8vo. 1542. L'Andria, 8vo. 1544.
27. GOVERNO della famiglia. 8vo. 1589.
28. HISTORIÆ Romanæ Scriptores. 8vo. 1511.

29. HOMERI Opera. 2 vols. 8vo. 1528, 1537.
30. HORATIUS. 8vo. 1503.
31. HYGINI poeticon. 1497, 1499.
32. JUSTINIANI B. Oratio. 4to. 1501.
33. LETTERE Volgari. 8vo. 1553.
34. LIBURNIO. N. Le Vulgare Elegantie, etc. 8vo. 1521.
35. LIVIUS. Folio. 1558, 1571, 1591.
36. LUCRETIUS. 8vo. 1550.
37. MANUTIUS P. de commitiis Romanorum. Folio. 1585, 1592.
38. MARTIALIS. 8vo. 1510, 1512.
39. MESUE G. I libri de i semplici. 8vo. 1589.
40. MURETI commentaria in Ep. Cic. 8vo. 1547.
41. NIZOLIUS M. Thesaurus Ciceronianus. Folio. 1591.
42. ORBECCHE, tragedia di G. Cynthio. 8vo. 1553.
43. OVIDII heroidum Epistolæ. 8vo. 1583.
44. PETRARCA. Le Rime. 8vo. 1504, 1507.
45. PHILO. 1498.
46. PHILOPONI J. Commentaria. Fol. 1535.
47. PHILOSTRATUS. Folio. 1504.
48. PICI. J. F. de Imaginatione. 4to. 1501.
49. PLINII Epist. 8vo. 1504.
50. RHODIGINI lectiones antiquæ. 8vo. 1559.

51. SALLUSTIUS. 8vo. 1564.

52. SEVERUS, Sulpitius. 1502.

53. TERENTIUS. 8vo. 1559, 1565.

54. THEMISTII opera. Folio. 1533.

55. THEOPHRASTUS. 1498.

56. THESAURUS Cornucopiæ. Folio. 1504.

57. VALERIUS Maximus. 8vo. 1512.

58. VARRO. 4to. 1498.

59. VIAGGIO da Venetia, etc. 8vo. 1541.

60. VITO N. dello stato delle Republiche. 4to.
    1591.

APPENDIX.

—◦◦◆◦◦—

CATALOGUES ISSUED BY
ALDUS MANUTIUS.

(See Vol. I., Page 23.)

—◦◦◆◦◦—

CATALOGUE OF 1498.

—◦◦◆◦◦—

LIBRI GRAECI IMPRESSI.

Hæc sunt græcorum uoluminum nomina, quæ in Thermis Aldi Romani Venetiis impressa sunt ad hunc usq; diem. s. primum octobris. M. IID. Nam cum quotidie aliquis peteret, qui nam græci libri formis excusi sint, ac quanti ueneant ad minimum, quod uel ipse scire cuperet, uel ad amicos id cupide elflagitantes mitteret, pertædebat toties idem scribere occupatissimum hominem.

In grammatica.

Erotemata Constantini Lascaris e regione cum interpretatione latina. Item de literis, ac diphthongis græcis. Item introductio quædam docens etiam sine magistro syllabas et dictiones græcas posse legere, tam paruis quam maiusculis scriptas characteribus. Item quo nam modo literæ et diphthongi græcæ ad nos ueniant. Item abbreuiationes quam plurimæ, quibus frequentissime græci utuntur. Item Pater noster. Aue Maria. Salue Regina. Credo in unum deum patrem omnipotentem. In principio erat uerbum. Item aurea carmina Pythagoræ. Item precepta Phocylidæ utilissima, omnia cum expositione latina e regione in uno uolumine. uenduntur marcellis quatuor.* (1494-5. 4to.)

Grammatica Vrbani utilissima ad declinanda nomina, pronomina, et uerba omnia tam lingua communi, quam aliis quatuor. Attica. Ionica. Dorica. Aeolica. cum regulis optimis et necessariis ita, ut nihil ferè sit prætermissum, quod introducere posse in græcam linguam uisum fuerit. Vbi etiam copiose tractatur de cæteris orationis partibus. Venditur non minoris marcellis quatuor. (1497, 4to.)

Canonismata quæ thesaurus et cornucopiæ appellantur dictionum difficilium, et maxime uerborum quæ apud Homerum. ex commentariis Eustathii, et aliorum grammaticorum per ordinem literarum. Aelii Dionysii de indeclinabilibus uerbis. Declinationes uerborum sum et eo, utilissimæ. De iis quæ sedere significant. Quot sint quæ ire signi-

---

* The *Marcellus* was a silver coin, named after Nicolo Marcellus, Doge of Venice in 1473, and was worth about 6·80 pence. The *Nummus Aureus Ducat* or *Zecchino* was worth 12·40 *Marcelli*, or about 7 shillings of our money. It should, however, be remembered that the value of Venetian gold, as compared with silver, was at the end of the 15th century only in the proportion of 11⅓ to 1.

ficant. Ex scriptis Herodiani excerpta de magno verbo scitu dignissima, et rara inventu. Ex scriptis eiusdem deductiones uerborum difficulter declinatorum. Chœrobosci ad eos qui in omnibus uerbis regulas quærunt et similitudines. Eiusdem in quibus ob malesonantiam attrahatur. n. litera. De anomalis et inæqualibus uerbis secundum ordinem alphabeti. Herodiani de inclinatis, et encliticis. et coencliticis dictiunculis. Ex scriptis Chœrobosci de iis quæ inclinantur, encliticísq;. Sine auctore de iis quæ inclinantur. Ex scriptis Ioannis grammatici de idiomatis. Eustathii de idiomatis quæ apud Homerum. Item de idiomatis, ex iis quæ a Corintho decerpta. De fœmininis nominibus, quæ desinunt in o magnum. omnia in uno uolumine. Venduntur minimo, nummo aureo et semis. (1496, folio.)

Grammatica doctissima et (pace aliorum dixerim) omnium utilissima Theodori Gazæ uiri ingenio et doctrina uel cum antiquissimis conferendi. Eiusdem de mensibus pulcherrimum opus. Item quatuor libri Appollonii de constructione. Omnia in uno uolumine. Veneunt aureo nummo, nec minoris. (1495, folio.)

Dictionarium græcum copiosissimum secundum ordinem Alphabeti cum interpretatione latina. Cyrilli opusculum de dictionibus, quæ uariato accentu mutant significatum secundum ordinem alphabeti cum interpretatione latina. Ammonius de differentia dictionum per literarum ordinem. Vetus instructio et denominationes perfectorum (sic) militum. Significata ταυ ῆ. Significata ταυ ως. Index oppido quam copiosus per litera-rum latinarum ordinem, quod est loco dictionarii latini copiosissimi cum interpretatione græca. Docet. n. latinas. dictiones feré omneis græce

dicere, et multas et multis modis. Omnes in uno
uolumine, minimum pretium est aureus nummus.
(1497, folio.)

In Poetica.

Theocriti eclogæ triginta. Hesiodi theogonia.
Eiusdem scutum Herculis. Eiusdem georgicorum
libri duo. Maximi Planudæ ex latino libro qui
Cato dicitur Sententiæ paræneticæ distichi. Caput
De inuidia. Theognidis Megarensis siculi Sententiæ
elegiacæ. Sententiæ perutiles monostichi per capita
ex uariis poetis. Aurea Carmina Pythagoræ.
Phocylidæ poema admonitorium utilissimum.
Carmina Sybillæ erythræeæ de christo IESV.
Differentia uocum. Omnia in uno uolumine.
Venduntur non minoris marcellis octo. (1495,
folio.)

Aristophanis cum antiquis commentariis Comœ-
diæ novem. Plutus. Nebulæ. Ranæ. Equites.
Acharnes. Vespæ. Aues. Pax. Contionatrices
fœminæ. Minimum pretium uenetiis, aurei
nummi duo et semis. (1498, folio.)

Musæi poetæ antiquissimi De Herone et
Leandro amantibus cum interpretatione latina.
uenditur, marcello. (No date, 4to.)

In logica.

Logica Aristotelis. i. organum. hoc est Porphyrii
introductio siue uniuersalia liber unus. Prædicamenta Aristotelis. liber unus. Perlhermenias liber
unus, siue sectiones sex. Priora resolutoria libri
duo. Posteriora resolutoria libri duo. Topica
libri octo. Elenchi libri duo. Omnes in uno
uolumine. uenduntur aureo et semis. (1495,
folio.)

In Philosophia. Primum uolumen.

Vita Aristotelis per Laertium et philoponum. et

uita Theophrasti. Aristotelis physicorum libri
octo. De cœlo libri quatuor. De generatione et
corruptione libri duo. Meteorologicorum libri
quatuor. De mundo ad Alexandrum liber unus.
et Philonis iudæi de mundo liber unus. Theophrasti de igne liber unus. De uentis liber unus.
De lapidibus liber unus. De signis aquarum et
uentorum incerti auctoris. Omnes in uno uolumine. uenduntur ad minimum nummis aureis
duobus. (1497, folio.)

Secundum uolumen.

De historia animalium libri octo. De partibus
animalium libri quatuor. De gressu animalium
liber unus. De anima libri tres. De sensu liber
unus. De memoria liber unus. De somno et
uigilia liber unus. De somniis liber unus. De
diuinatione per somnium, liber unus. De motu
animalium liber unus. De generatione animaliun,
libri quinq;. De longitudine et breuitate uitæ
liber unus. De iuuentute et senectute, et respira-
tione, et uita et morte libri tres. De spiritu liber
unus. De coloribus liber unus. Physiognomi-
corum liber unus. De mirabilibus auditionibus
liber unus. De Xenophanis Zenonis. et Gorgiæ
opinionibus, liber unus. De indiuisibilibus lineis,
liber unus. Theophrasti de piscibus liber unus.
De uertigine oculorum liber unus. De laboribus,
liber unus. De odoribus, liber unus. De sudori-
bus, liber unus. omnes in uno uolumine. minimum
pretium Venetiis nummi aurei duo et semis.
(1497, folio.)

Tertium Volumen.

Theophastri de historia plantarum, libri decem.
Eiusdem de causis plantarum libri sex. Aristotelis problematum sectiones duodequadraginta.

Alexandri aphrodisiensis problematum libri duo. Aristotelis mechanicorum liber unus. Eiusdem metaphysicorum libri quatuordecim. Theophastri metaphysicorum liber unus. Omnes in uno uolumine. minimum pretium nummi aurei, tres. (1497, folio.)

Quartum Volumen.

Aristotelis magnorum moralium ad Nicomachum patrem libri duo. Ethicorum ad Eudemum discipulum libri octo. Ethicorum ad Nicomachum filium libri decem. Oeconomicorum libri duo. Politicorum libri octo. omnes in eodem uolumine. minimum pretium nummi aurei duo. (1498, folio.)

In sacra scriptura.

Psalterium græcum. uenditur marcellis quatuor. (No date, 4to.)

Officium in honorem Beatissimæ uirginis cum psalmis penitentialibus è latino in græcum. uenditur Marcellis duobus. (1497, 8vo.)

CATALOGUE OF 1503.

ALDVS STVDIOSIS. S.

LIBRORVM et græcorum : et latinorum nomina, quot-quot in hunc usq; diem excudendos curauimus, scire uos uoluimus. Vbi etiam quædam de libris singulis, tanquam eorum argumenta dicuntur: ut inde quid singulo quoq; libro tractatur : facile cognoscatís. Quod ideo factum est : quia cum undiq; ad nos scribatur: qui nam libri cura nostra excusi sint : sic satisfaciamus : cum aliter, propter summas occupationes nostras : non liceat.

LIBRI GRAECI.

Erotemata Constantini Lascaris tribus libris :
&c. Inest etiam perbreuis ad hebraicam linguam
introductio. (No date, 4to.)

Grammatica Vrbani utilissima, &c. (1497,
4to.

Canonismata : quæ thesaurus, & cornucopiæ
appellantur dictionum difficilium, &c. (1496,
folio.)

Grammatica doctissima : & (pace aliorum
dixerim) omnium utilissima Theodori Gazæ, &c.
(1495, folio.)

Dictionarium græcum, &c. (1497, folio.)

Theocriti eclogæ triginta. Hesiodi theogonia.
Euisdem scutum Herculis. Eiusdem georgicorum
libri duo, &c. (1495, folio.)

Aristophanis cum antiquis commentariis Comœ-
diæ nouem, &c. (1498, folio.)

Musæi poetæ antiquissimi De Herone : &
Leandro amantibus opusculum cum interpretatione
latina. (No date, 4to.)

Logica Aristotelis, quod organum græce dicitur,
&c. (1495, folio.)

. Primum uolumen in philosophia, &c. (1497,
folio.)

Secundum, &c. (1497, folio.)

Tertium, &c. (1497, folio.)

Quartum, &c. (1498, folio.)

Psalterium græcum. (No date, 4to.)

Officium in honorem Beatissimæ uirginis cum
psalmis penitentialibus e latino in græcum. (1497,
8vo.)

Epistolarum mille et septuaginta trium uolumen,
&c. (1499, 2 vols. 4to.)

Gregorii Nazanzeni opusculum, ubi philoso-
phatur, &c. (1504, 4to.)

Nonni poetæ Panopolitani Paraphrasis totius
historiæ Euangelicæ secundum Ioannem carmine
heroico excelenti......sunt autem carminum tria
millia : et trecenta : ac quinq ; et triginta. habent
latinam interpretationem e regione,* &c.

Dioscorides, &c. Nicandri Colophonii poetæ
theriaca cum commentariis. Eiusdem Alexipharmaca cum commentariis. (1499, folio.)

Leontii Mechanici de Sphæræ Arati constructione. Arati Solensis phænomena cum commentariis Theonis. Procli Diadochi sphæra : et
græce : et latine. (1499, folio.)

Iulii pollucis uocabularium, &c. (1502, folio.)

Stephanus de urbibus opus perquam utile, &c.
(1502, folio.)

Thucydides de bello inter Peloponnenses : et
Athenienses, libri octo, &c. (1502, folio.)

Herodoti libri nouem, quibus musarum......
indita ab eo nomina, &c. (1502, folio.)

Luciani opuscula. 171......Icones quinque et
sexaginta Philostrati........Eiusdem heroica........
Icones iunioris Philostrati duodeuiginti..... Item
Enarrationes Callistrati in statuas quatuordecim.
Necnon Philostrati uitæ sophistarum. 58. (1503,
folio.)

Paralipomena Xenophontis. i. historia græcarum
rerum, quas prætermisit Thucydides : libris septem.
Gemistonis, qui et Pletho dicitur ; historiæ græcæ
derelictæ a Xenophonte, duobus libris. Herodianus. (1503, folio.)

---

* This Latin version of Nonnus is here announced
in anticipation of its publication, which, however,
never took place.

Philostrati de uita Apollonii Tyanei libri octo
......Iidem libri latini......Eusebius contra Hieroclem.......Idem latinus. (1501, folio.)

Ammonius in praedicamenta Aristotelis. Idem
in librum περὶ ἑρμηνείας i. de interpretatione.
Margentinus in eundm. (1503, folio.)

Ioannes grammaticus in priora : et posteriora
resolutoria Aristotelis. (1504, folio.)

Sophoclis tragœdiæ septem, in formam Enchiridii. (1502, 8vo.)

Euripidis tragœdiæ duodeuiginti in formam
Enchiridii. (1503, 2 vqls., 8vo.)

Epigrammata græca in enchiridii formam a
diuersis composita. (1503, 8vo.)

Libros græcos, qui secuntur : et si ab aliis impressi sunt ; tamen, quia in bibliopolio nostro
habentur uenales : adnotauimus. sunt uero hi.

Etymologicum magnum. (*Venetiis*, 1499, folio.)

Simplicius predicamenta Aristotelis. (*Ibid*, 1499,
folio.)

Ammonius in prædicabilia Porphyrii. (*Ibid*,
1500, folio.)

Apollonius de Argonautis cum commentariis.
(*Florentiae*, 1496, 4to.)

Homeri libri. 48. et uita eius ex Plutarcho.
Herodoto, et Dione. (*Ibid*, 1488, 2 vols., folio.)

Suidas uocabularium magnum. (*Mediolani*,
1499, folio.)

Libri latini.

Sedulii libri......Prudentii opera. (1501-2, 2
vols., 4to.)

Opera Politiani. (1498, folio.)

Iulii firmici Astronomicorum libri octo integri :
et emendati. Allatum n. fuit exemplar ex Scythia.
Marci Manlii astronomicorum libri quinqc ; heroico

carmine. Arati phænomena, latine......Eadem
græca......Theonis commentaria in Aratum, græce.
Procli Sphæra græce. Eadem latina Thoma
Linacro Britanno interprete. (1499, folio.)
Nicolai Perotti Cornucopiæ. (1499, folio.)
Iamblichus......Proclus......Porphyrius. (1497,
folio.)
Lucretius emendatus. (1500, 4to.)
Georgii Vallæ opus ingens de expetendis et
fugiendis rebus. (1501, 2 vols., folio.)
Grammaticæ institutiones nostræ de grammatices
et orationis partibus. De constructione: ubi in
Patronymicis ostendimus necessariam esse liter-
arum græcarum cognitionem hominibus nostris.
tum perbreuis introductio ad græcam et herbrai-
cam linguam. (1501, 4to.)
Origenes in Genesin. Exodum. Leuiticum.
Numeros. Iesum Naue. in libros Iudicum opus
utilissimum, diuo Hieronymo interprete. (1503,
folio.)
Bessarionis Cardinalis Niceni, libri quatuor in
calumniatorem Platonis. (1503, folio.)
Aristoteles de animalibus. Theophastrus de
Plantis. Problemata Aristotelis et Alexandri
aphrodisiei: Theodoro Gaza interprete. (1504,
folio.)
Laurentii Maioli Genuensis epiphyllides in
dialecticis: ubi sunt capita. 18. (1497, 4to.)
Diuæ Catherinæ Senensis epistolæ. 359. (1500,
folio.)

Libelli portatiles in formam enchiridii.

Vergilius. (1501.) Horatius. (1501.) Ouidius
tribus uoluminibus. (1502.) Statius. (1502.)
Lucanus. (1502.) Martialis. (1501.) Valerius
Maxim. (1502.) Dantes. (1502.) Petrarcha.

(1501.)   Epistolæ   familiares.   (1502.)   M.   T.
Iuuenalis et Persi.   (1501.)   Catullus. Tibullus.
Propertius.   (1502.)

Aldus has here inserted in his own handwriting:

Pantanus.

Ja. Aurelius.

Op. Bembi.

Hos ad hunc usq; diem excudendos libros
curauimus.   Mox uero daturi sumus Demosthenis
orationes cum argumentis Libanii : et commentariis
in 3 (*Orationibus*) Item Hermogenis Rhetorica
cum commentariis.   Commentarios etiam in opera
Aristotelis. tum Platonis opera : Pausaniam Omnia
Plutarchi : et cætera, quæ desyderantur : etiam
in medicina, et mathematicis : quemadmodum a
principio polliciti sumus : uiuam modo. et licet
misera hæc tempora aduersentur : tamen, quia
non cedimus malis : sed imus contra audentiores :
ferendo uincemus.   Quandoquidem labor omnia
uincit improbus.   Quod si, qd'iandiu parturimus :
aliquando pariemus : maximis omnes beneficiis
afficiemini : nec pœnitebit hisce natos esse tem-
poribus.   Valete : meq; de hac re : ut puto
facitis : Amate.   Debetis enim, quoniam suppedi-
tando uobis optimos quosq; libros : assidua, et
incredibili cura : ac summis laboribus : pro
ministro sum uobis a manu.   Equidem in hac re
fungor uice cotis : acutum reddere quæ ſcirum
ualet exors ipsa secandi.   Facile enim uos mea
opera euadetis in summos uiros. ipse uero tantum
suscipiam uos : ut indoctus pater exultans doctrina, et excellentia filiorum.   Sit ita sane.   Vnum

pro cunctis dabitur caput. Venetiis. XXII. Iunii. M. DIII.

Aldus has here inserted in his own handwriting:

Demosthenis orationes cum Commentariis.

Homerus in parua forma.

Quintus.

Vita et fabellae Aesopi cum interpretatione latina, &c.

CATALOGUE OF 1513.

(This is a copy of the Catalogue of 1503 as far as the Latin books, page 37, but the Nonnus appears only as a Greek work, Aldus having given up the idea of publishing the Latin version. Bolzani's Greek Grammar has also disappeared, together with the Ancient Astronomers, 1499.)

The Catalogue continues thus :—

Homeri libri. 48. et uita eius ex Plutarcho, Herodoto, et Dione, forma enchiridij. 2 vols.

Quintus Calaber de derelictis ab Homero, quatuordecim libris forma enchiridij.

Orationes Demosthenis.

Vlpiani Commentaria.

Moralia Plutarchi.

Phornutus .....Aesopus......Gabrias.

Liber duodecim Rhetorum de arte rhetorica.

In Aphthonij progymnasmata commentarij.

Grammatica Chrysoloræ, cum libro quarto Theodori de constructione. cum sententijs monostichis per ordinem alphabeti ex uarijs poetis forma enchiridij.

Pindarus cum Callimacho. Dionysio de situ orbis. Lycophrone.

Isocratis orationes, et Alcidamantis contra dicendi magistros. et Gorgiæ de laudibus Helenæ.

Aristidis de laudibus Athenarum, et de laudibus urbis Romæ.

Aeschinis orationes cum Lysiæ orationibus. Alcidamantis. Anthistenis. Demadis. Andocidis. Isæi. Dinarchi. Antiphontis. Lycurgi. Gorgiæ. Lesbonactis. Herodis. Aeschinis uita. Lysiæ uita.

Platonis opera.

Suidas denuo impressus.

Alexander Aphrodisieus in topica Aristotelis.

Libros græcos, qui sequuntur, et si ab alijs impressi sunt, tamen, quia in bibliopolio nostro habentur uenales, adnotauimus. sunt uero hi.

Etymologicum magnum.

Simplicius in prædicamenta Aristotelis.

Ammonius in prædicabilia Porphyrij.

Apollonius de Argonautis cum commentarijs.

LIBRI LATINI.

Opera Politiani.

Iulii firmici Astronomicorum, libri octo.

Nicolai Perotti Sypontini Cornucopiæ, &c. Varronis libri de lingua Latina, et Analogia. Sextus Pompeius Festus. Nonius Marcellus, in quo multa addita, non ante impressa.

Grammaticæ institutiones nostræ latinæ, nam græcas adhuc premimus, libris quatuor.

Bessarionis Cardinalis Niceni, libri quatuor in calumniatorem Platonis.

Aristoteles de animalibus. Theophrastus de Plantis. Problemata Aristotelis, et Alexandri aphrodisiei, Theodoro Gaza interprete.

Prouerbia Erasmi.

Libelli forma enchiridij.

Vergilius.
Horatius.
Catullus. Tibullus. Propertius.
Ouidius tribus uoluminibus.
Lucanus.
Statius.
Martialis.
Pontani Vrania.
Strozij poetæ ferrarienses, pater. et filius.
Iuuenalis, et Persius.
Hecuba Erasmi.
M. Tullij Epistolæ familiares.
Eiusdem Epistolæ ad Atticum.
Sallustius.
Commentaria Cæsaris.
Valerius Maximus.
Epistolæ Plinij.
Dantes.
Petrarcha.
Horæ Beatæ Virginis per quam parua forma.
VENETIIS. XXIIII. Nouembris. M. D. XIII.

[A fourth Catalogue, dated 1563, is given by Renouard, but it has no value.]

INDEX TO AUTHORS.

(The various Editions of the same Author will be found under the dates named.)

A.

ABDUENSIS Ferdinandi Opera. 1546.

Academia Veneta : Sommario delle sue opere. 1558. Summa librorum, &c. 1559.

Adeodatus Senensis. 1552.

Adriani Card. Venatio, 1505. et cum Gratio. 1534.

Aegineta Paulus. 1528. 53. 58.

Aeliani Epistolae : in Collectione Epistolarum graecarum. 1499.

Aelius Dionysius de indeclinabilibus verbis, &c. In Thes. Cornucopiae. 1496.

Aelius Spartianus : cum Egnatio. 1516. 19.

Aemilius Probus : cum Justino. 1522.

Aeneae Epistolae : in Collectione Epistolarum graecarum. 1499.

Aeschinis Epistolae : in Collectione Epistolarum graecarum. 1499. Orationes : cum Oratoribus graecis. 1513. trad. in Ital. 1554. 57.

Aeschylus. 1518.

Aetius Amidenus. 1534.

Albertus Leo Bapt. De Legato Pontificio. 1558.

Alciatus Andreas. 1546.

Alcidamantis Orationes : cum Oratoribus graecis. 1513. & cum Isocrate. 13. 34.

Alcinoi liber de doctrina Platonis : cum Jamblico. 1497. 1516. cum Apulejo. 1521.

Alciphronis Epistolae : in Collectione Epistolarum graecarum. 1499.

VOL. III.   *a*

C.

D.

F.

Hesiodi Theogonia,—Scutum Herculis,—Georgicon libri duo : cum Theocrito. 1495.
Hesychius. 1514.
D. Hieronymus, 1562, 64, 65, 66, Origenis interpres, 1503.
Hilario, Monachus Veronensis, Hermogenis interpres : in Rhetor. gr. lat. versis. 1523.
Hippocratis Epistolae : in Collectione Epistolar. graecar. 1499, Opera, 1526, Methodus in ejus Aphorismos 1550.
A Hirtius : cum Caesare, 1513, &c.
Historia delle cose occorse in Inghilterra, 1558.
Historiae Augustae Scriptores, 1516, 19.
Homeri Ilias & Odyssea, Sine anno, et 1504, 17, 24.
Homerocentra : cum Poetis christianis, 1501.
Horae B. M. Virginis, 1497, 1505, 1521, absque anno.
Horapollu : cum AEsopo, 1505.
Horatius, 1501, 09, 19, 27, Lambini, 66, M. Ant. Mureti. 55, 59, 61, 64, 66. 70,
Hosius Stanislaus, 1565.
Huarte Giovanni, 1582, 86, 90.

I.

Jamblichus de Mysteriis, 1497, 1516.
Jasonis de Nores in Horat. Interpr. 1553.
Index Librorum Aldinae officinae. 1498, 1503, 13, 63.
Index Librorum prohibitorum, 1564.
Institutioni dell'Imperio contenute nella Bolla d'oro, trad. da Luca Contile, 1558.
Interiano Giorgio, 1502.
Intronati : Il Sacrifizio, 1550.
Joannes Grammaticus, 1504, 27, 34, in Thesauro Cornuc. 1496, In Grammatica Lascaris, 1512, 40, 57, cum Olympiodoro, 51, cum Dictionario graeco. 1524.
Joannis Evangelium, gr. l. In Gram. Lascaris Appen-

M.

T.

THE END.